# Praise for Freak the Mighty:

"A small classic, funny-sad, page-turning and memorable... Suspenseful, touching and swiftly persuasive about its most unusual central characters, this remarkable book takes you through dark territory, but is written with humour and simplicity. It celebrates language, loyalty and imagination, and leaves you smiling."

*The Sunday Times*

"As funny as it is touching and convincing."

*The Guardian*

"Moving and inspirational."

*Funday Times*

"Uplifting."

*The Bookseller*

"A heart-breaking tale. *Freak the Mighty* offers everything you could possibly wish for in a novel... Get reading now and prepare to sob your heart out."

*Red House*

"This is an exciting and emotional read. Highly recommended."

*Carousel*

# FREAK the MIGHTY

## RODMAN PHILBRICK

USBORNE

This edition first published in the UK in 2004 by Usborne Publishing Ltd.,
Usborne House, 83-85 Saffron Hill, London EC1N 8RT, England.
www.usborne.com

Text copyright © 1993 by Rodman Philbrick.
Published by arrangement with Scholastic Inc.,
557 Broadway, New York, NY 10012, USA

Cover copyright © Usborne Publishing Ltd., 2006.

A CIP catalogue record for this book is available from the British Library.

JFMAMJJAS ND/07

Printed in Great Britain.

To the real Kevin,
and the real Gwen, with love.

# The Unvanquished Truth 1

I never had a brain until Freak came along and let me borrow his for a while, and that's the truth, the whole truth. The unvanquished truth, is how Freak would say it, and for a long time it was him who did the talking. Except I had a way of saying things with my fists and my feet even before we became Freak the Mighty, slaying dragons and fools and walking high above the world.

Called me Kicker for a time – this was day care, the year Gram and Grim took me over – and I had a thing about booting anyone who dared to touch me. Because they were *always* trying to throw a hug on me, like it was a medicine I needed.

Gram and Grim, bless their pointed little heads, they're my mother's people, *her* parents, and they figured whoa! better put this little critter with other little critters his own age, maybe it will improve his temper.

Yeah, right! Instead, what happened, I invented games like kick-boxing and kick-knees and kick-faces and kick-teachers, and kick-the-other-little-day-care-critters, because I knew what a rotten lie that hug stuff was. Oh, I *knew*.

That's when I got my first look at Freak, that year of the phoney hugs. He didn't look so different back then, we were all of us pretty small, right? But he wasn't in the playroom with us every day, just now and then he'd show up. Looking sort of fierce is how I remember him. Except later it was Freak himself who taught me that remembering is a great invention of the mind, and if you try hard enough you can remember anything, whether it really happened or not.

So maybe he wasn't really all *that* fierce in day care, except I'm pretty sure he did hit a kid with his crutch once, whacked the little brat pretty good. And for some reason little Kicker never got around to kicking little Freak.

Maybe it was those crutches kept me from lashing out at him, man those crutches were cool. I wanted a pair for myself. And when little Freak showed up one day with these shiny braces strapped to his crooked legs, metal tubes right up to his hips, why those were even *more* cool than crutches.

"I'm Robot Man," little Freak would go, making these weird robot noises as he humped himself around the playground. *Rrrr. . .rrr. . .rrr. . .*like he had robot motors inside his legs, going *rrrrr. . .rrrr . . .rrrr,* and this look, like don't mess with me, man, maybe I got a laser cannon hidden inside these leg braces, smoke a hole right through you. No question, Freak was hooked on robots even back then, this little guy two feet tall, and already he knew what he wanted.

Then for a long time I never saw Freak any more, one day he just never came back to day care, and the next thing I remember I'm like in the third grade or something and I catch a glimpse of this yellow-haired kid scowling at me from one of those cripple vans. Man, they were death-ray eyes, and I think, hey, that's him, the robot boy, and it was like whoa! because I'd forgotten all about him, day care was a blank place in my head, and nobody had called me Kicker for a long time.

Mad Max they were calling me, or Max Factor, or this one butthead in L.D. class called me Maxi Pad, until I persuaded him otherwise. Gram and Grim always called me Maxwell, though, which is supposed to be my real name, and sometimes I hated that worst of all. Maxwell, ugh.

Grim out in the kitchen one night, after supper whispering to Gram had she noticed how much Maxwell was getting to look like *Him*? Which is the way he always talked about my father, who has married his dear departed daughter and produced, eek eek, Maxwell. Grim never says my father's name, just *Him*, like his name is too scary to say.

It's more than just the way Maxwell resembles him, Grim says that night in the kitchen, the boy is *like* him, we'd better watch out, you never know what he might do while we're sleeping. Like his father did. And Gram right away shushes him and says don't ever say that, because little pictures have big ears, which makes me run to the mirror to see if it is my ears made me look like *Him*.

What a butthead, huh?

Well, I *was* a butthead, because like I said, I never had a brain until Freak moved down the street. The summer before eighth grade, right? That's the summer I grew so fast that Grim said we'd best let the boy go barefoot, he's exploding out of his shoes. That barefoot summer when I fell down a lot, and the weirdo robot boy with his white-yellow hair and his weird fierce eyes moved into the duplex down the block with his beautiful brown-haired mum, the Fair Gwen of Air.

Only a falling-down goon would think that was her real name, right?

Like I said.

Are you paying attention here? Because you don't even know yet how we got to be Freak the Mighty. Which was pretty cool, even if I do say so myself.

# 2 Up from the Down Under

That summer, let's see, I'm still living in the basement, my own private down under, in the little room Grim built for me there. Glued up this cheap panelling, right? It sort of buckles away from the concrete cellar walls, a regular ripple effect, but do I complain about the crummy panelling, or the rug that smells like low tide? I do not. Because I *like* it in the down under, got the place all to myself and no fear of Gram sticking her head in the door and saying Maxwell dear, what *are* you doing?

Not that I ever *do* much of anything. Grim has it fixed in his head I'm at a dangerous age and they need to keep me under observation. Like I might make bombs or start a fire. Or whack out the local pets with my trusty slingshot or whatever – except I never *had* a slingshot, it was Grim who had one when he was my age. The proof is right there in the family photo album. You can see this blurry little miniature Grim with no front teeth, grinning at the camera and yanking back on his prehistoric slingshot. Good for whacking mastodons, probably. "Just proper targets," Grim says, closing up the photo album, end of discussion. Like, oops, better hide the evidence. Don't want to give the dangerous boy any ideas.

Not that I *have* any ideas. My brain is vacant, okay? I'm just this critter hiding out in the basement, drooling in my comic books or whatever. All right, I never actually *drool*, but you get the picture.

Anyhow, this is the first day of July, already counting down for the Fourth and wondering where I can get an M80, which is supposed to have the explosive power of a quarter stick of dynamite or something, and when it goes off your heart thuds to a stop for a microsecond, *wham*. Which is probably what Grim is afraid of, eek eek, Maxwell armed with dynamite.

So finally I get bored in the down under and I'm hanging out in the so-called back yard, your basic chunk of chain-link heaven. Grim keeps this crummy little mower in the shed, but what's the point of mowing dirt, right? Okay, I'm out there messing around and that's when I see the moving van. Not your mainstream, nationwide, brand-name mover, either, just some cheapo local outfit. These big bearded dudes in their sweaty undershirts lugging stuff into the duplex half that's been vacant since last Christmas, when the dope fiend who lived there finally got busted.

At first I'm thinking the dope fiend is back, he's out of jail or whatever, and he's moving his stuff back in. Then I see the Fair Gwen. Not that I knew her name, that was a little while later. At first she's a glimpse, caught her going between the van and the front door, talking to the beards. I'm thinking, *hey I know her*, and then I'm thinking, *no way, butthead, no way you'd know a female that beautiful*.

Because she looks like some kind of movie star. Wearing these old jeans and a baggy T-shirt, and her long hair is tied back and she's probably sweating, but she *still* looks like a movie star. Like she has this glow, a secret spotlight that follows her around and makes her eyes light up.

And I'm thinking, well *this* improves the old neighbourhood. You're thinking, yeah right, the goon is barely out of seventh grade, who does he think he is? All I'm saying, the Fair Gwen had star quality, and even a total moron can see it. And the reason she looked familiar is, I must have seen her bringing Freak to day care, way back in the dark ages, because the next thing I notice is this crippled-up yellow-haired midget kid strutting around the sidewalk, giving orders to the beards.

He's going: "Hey you, Doofus! Yeah, you with the hairy face, take it easy with that box. That box contains a computer, you know what a computer is?"

I can't believe it. By then I'm sneaking along the street to see what's going on, and there's this weird-looking dude, he's got a normal-sized head, but the rest of him is shorter than a yardstick and kind of twisted in a way that means he can't stand up straight and makes his chest puff out, and he's waving his crutches around and yelling up at the movers.

"Hey, Gwen," one of the beards says, "can't you give this kid a pill or something? He's driving us nuts."

So Gwen comes out of the house and pushes the hair out of her big brown eyes and she goes, "Kevin, go play in the back yard, okay?"

"But my computer."

"Your computer is fine. Leave the men alone. They'll be done soon and then we can have lunch."

By this time I'm hunkering along in front of the place, trying to maintain a casual attitude, except like I said my feet are going wild that year and I keep tripping over everything. Cracks in the sidewalk, ants on the sidewalk, shadows, anything.

Then the strange little dude jerks himself around and he catches sight of me and he lifts a crutch and points it up at my heart and he goes, "Identify yourself, earthling."

I'm busy keeping my feet from tripping and don't get that he means me.

"I said identify yourself, earthling, or suffer the consequences."

I'm like, what? And before I can decide whether or not to tell him my name, or *which* name, because by now I recognize him as the weird little robot kid from day care and maybe he remembers me as Kicker, anyhow before I can say a word he pulls the trigger on that crutch and makes a weapon noise, and he goes, "Then die, earthling, die!"

I motor out of there without saying a word. Because I'm pretty sure he really means it. The way he points that crutch is only part of it. You have to see the look in his eye. Man, that little dude really hates me.

He *wants* me to die.

# American Flyer 3

Okay, back to the down under, right? My room in the basement. Scuttle into your dim hole in the ground, Maxwell dear. Big goon like you, growing about an inch a day, and this midget kid, this crippled little humanoid, he actually *scared* you. Not the kind of scare that makes your knee bones feel like water, more the kind of scare where you go whoa! I don't understand this, I don't get it, what's going on?

Like calling me "earthling". Which by itself is pretty weird, right? I already mentioned a few of the names I've been called, but until the robot boy showed up, nobody had ever called me *earthling*, and so I'm lying on my mattress there in the great down under, and it comes to me that he's right, I *am* an earthling, we're all of us earthlings, but we don't call each other earthling. No need. Because it's the same thing that in this country we're all Americans, but we don't go around to people and say, "Excuse me, American, can you tell me how to get to the nearest 7 Eleven?"

So I'm thinking about that for a while, lying there in the cellar dark, and pretty soon the down under starts to get small, like the walls are shrinking, and I go up the bulkhead stairs into the back yard and find a place where I can check it out.

There's this one scraggly tree behind the little freak's house, right? Like a stick in the ground with a few wimped-out branches. And there he is, hardly any bigger now than he was in day care, and he's standing there waving his crutch up at the tree.

I kind of slide over to the chain-link fence, get a better angle on the scene. What's he *doing* whacking at that crummy tree? Trying to jump up and hit this branch with his little crutch, and he's mad, hopping mad. Only he can't really jump, he just makes this jumping kind of motion. His feet never leave the ground.

Then what he does, he throws down the crutch and he gets down on his hands and knees and crawls back to his house. If you didn't know, you would think he was a kindergarten creeper who forgot how to walk, he's that small. And he crawls real good, better than he can walk. Before you know it, he's dragging this wagon out from under the steps.

Rusty red thing, one of those old American Flyer models. Anyhow, the little freak is tugging it backwards, a few inches at a time. Chugging along until he gets that little wagon under the tree. Next thing he picks up his crutch and he climbs in the wagon and he stands up and he's whacking the tree again.

By now I've figured out that there's something stuck up in the branches and he wants to get it down. This small, bright-coloured thing, looks like a piece of folded paper. Whatever it is, that paper thing, he wants it real bad, but even with the wagon there's no way he can reach it. No way.

So I go over there to his back yard, trying to be really quiet, but I'm no good at sneaking up, not with these humongous feet, and he turns and faces me with that crutch raised up like he's ready to hit the grand slam on my head.

He wants to say something, you can tell that much, but he's so mad, he's all huffed up and the noise he makes, it could be from a dog or something, and he sounds like he can hardly breathe.

What I do, I keep out of range of that crutch and just reach up and pick the paper thing right out of the tree. Except it's not a paper thing. It's a plastic bird, light as a feather. I have to hold it real careful or it might break, that's how flimsy it is.

I go, "You want this back or what?"

The little freak is staring at me bug-eyed, and he goes, "Oh, it talks."

I give him the bird-thing. "What is it, like a model airplane or something?"

You can tell he's real happy to have the bird-thing back, and his face isn't quite so fierce. He sits down in the wagon, and he goes, "This is an ornithopter. An ornithopter is defined as an experimental device propelled by flapping wings. Or you could say that an ornithopter is just a big word for mechanical bird."

That's how he talked, like right out of a dictionary. So smart you can hardly believe it. While he's talking he's winding up the bird-thing. There's this elastic band inside, and he goes, "Observe and be amazed, earthling," and then he lets it go, and you know what? I *am* amazed, because it does fly just like a little bird, flitting up and down and around, higher than I can reach.

I chase after the thing until it boinks against the scrawny tree trunk and I bring it back to him and he winds it up again and makes it fly. We keep doing that, it must be for almost an hour, until finally the elastic breaks. I figure that's it, end of ornithopter, but he says something like, "All mechanical objects require periodic maintenance. We'll schedule installation of a new propulsion unit as soon as the Fair Gwen of Air gets a replacement."

Even though I'm not sure what he means, I go, "That's cool."

"You live around here, earthling?"

"Over there." I point out the house. "In the down under."

He goes, "What?" and I figure it's easier to show him than explain all about Gram and Grim and the room in the cellar, so I pick up the handle to the American Flyer Wagon and I tow him over.

It's real easy, he doesn't weigh much and I'm pretty sure I remember looking back and seeing him sitting up in the wagon happy as can be, like he's really enjoying the ride and not embarrassed to have me pulling him around.

But like Freak says later in this book, you can remember anything, whether it happened or not. All I'm really sure of is he never hit me with that crutch.

# 4 What Frightened the Fair Gwen

Freak's not in my room for ten minutes before he sets me straight on the Fair Gwen. He's able to hump down the steps by himself, except it makes him sort of out of breath, you can hear him wheezing or I guess you'd call it panting, like a dog does on a hot day. He gets into my room and I close the bulkhead door, and he goes, "Cool. You get to live down here all by yourself?"

"I eat upstairs with Grim and Gram."

Freak works himself up onto the foot of my bed and uses a pillow to make himself comfortable. It's pretty dim down here, only the daylight from one basement window, but it catches him just right and makes his eyes shine. "Gram must be your grandmother," he says. "Grim would be, I suppose, a sobriquet for your grandfather, based on his demeanour."

16

I go, "Huh?"

Freak grins and pushes back his yellow hair, and he goes, "Pardon my vocabulary. Sobriquet means 'nickname', and demeanour means 'expression'. I merely postulated that you call your grandfather 'Grim' because he's grim. Postulate means—"

"I know," I say. Which is a lie, except I can guess what he means, figure it out that way. "So how come you call your mom 'Fair Gwen of Air', is that a nickname?"

Freak is shaking his head. I can see he's trying not to let on that he's laughing inside. "Guinevere," he finally says, catching his breath. "The Fair Guinevere, from the legend of King Arthur. You know about King Arthur, right?"

I shrug. The only King Arthur I know is the brand of flour Gram uses, and if I say that I'll *really* sound like a butthead.

He goes, "My mom's name is Gwen, so sometimes I call her the Fair Guinevere or the Fair Gwen. King Arthur was the first king of England, way back when there were still dragons and monsters in the world. Arthur was this wimpy little kid, an orphan, and there was this magic sword stuck in a big stone, okay? The old king had died, and whoever could pull the sword from the stone

**17**

proved he was the next king. All these big tough dudes came from all over to yank at the sword and they couldn't budge it. One day this wimpy little kid tried it when nobody was looking and the sword slipped out like it was stuck in butter."

"So he was the king, this little kid?"

Freak nods, he's really into this story, and he's making shapes in the air with his hands. This is the first time for me, hearing Freak really talk, and right away I know one thing: When he's talking, you can't take your eyes off of him. His hands are moving, and it's like he's really seeing it, this story about an old king.

"Arthur's magical sword is called Excalibur, and the Fair Guinevere is this pretty girl who becomes his queen. 'Fair' in those days meant the same as 'beautiful' does now. Anyhow, Arthur got bored just sitting around, so he invited all the knights of England to come live in the castle. They all ate supper at this round table, which is why they were called the Knights of the Round Table. Every now and then King Arthur would send them off on a special secret mission, which in the old days they called a 'quest'. They had to slay dragons and monsters and evil knights. I assume you know what a knight wears into battle?"

I think so, but I like hearing Freak talk, so I go, "Better tell me," and that's when I find out why he's so interested in some clanky old knights.

Because Freak really lights up and he goes, "The knights were like the first human version of robots. They wore this metal armour to protect them and make them invincible. When I get my stuff unpacked I'll show you the pictures. It's pretty amazing, really, that hundreds of years before they had computers they were already attempting to exceed the design limitations of the human body."

I go, "Huh?" and Freak sort of chuckles to himself, like he expected me to go "Huh?" and he says, "The design limitations of the human body. You know, like we're not bullet-proof and we can't crush rocks with our bare hands, and if we touch a hot stove we get burned. King Arthur wanted to *improve* his men, so he made them armour-plated. Then he programmed them to go out and do these quests, slay the dragons and so on, which is sort of how they program robots right now."

I go, "I thought there weren't any real robots. Just in the movies."

Boy does that make his eyes blaze. Like whoa! talk about laser beams! He's like *fuming*, so upset he can hardly talk.

Finally he gets control of himself and he goes, "I suppose I must make allowances for your ignorance. On the subject of robots you are clearly misinformed. Robots are not just in the movies. Robotics, the science of designing and building functional robots, is a *huge* industry. There are *thousands* of robot units presently in use. *Millions* of them. They don't look like the robots you see in movies, of course, because they're designed according to function. Many robotic devices are in fact sophisticated assembly units, machines that put together cars and trucks and computers. For instance, the space shuttle has a robot arm."

"Right," I say. "I saw that on TV."

Freak sighs and rolls his eyes. "Ah, yes," he says. "Television, the opiate of the massives."

For about the eleventh time I go, "Huh?"

"Opiate, a drug," he says. "Massive, that means large and heavy. Thus television is the drug of fat heads. Opiate of the massives."

"You don't have a TV?"

"Of course I have a television," he says. "How else would I watch *Star Trek*? Matter of fact, I watch *tons* of tube but I also read tons of books so I can figure out what's true and what's fake, which isn't always easy. Books are like truth serum – if you don't read, you can't figure out what's real."

This time I don't say *huh* because then I might have to explain how I'm an L.D., and reading books is the last thing I want to do, right after trimming my toenails with a lawn mower, gargling nails, and eating worms for breakfast. Of course Freak has probably already guessed I'm a learning disabled, because he's had a look around my room and it isn't exactly the public library.

"I'll lend you some of my books," he says.

"Cool," I say, like it's what I've been waiting for, another chance to prove I'm a butthead.

Then we both hear it at the same time, this voice calling his name and sounding real worried.

"The Fair Gwen," he says. "I gotta beam out of here."

I go up and open the bulkhead door and his mother is in the back yard and she's looking at the little red wagon. She catches sight of me coming up out of the down under and it's like somebody shot her. Like she's scared out of her mind. "Kevin?" she says. "I'm looking for a little boy."

Freak is huffing and puffing as he humps himself up the steps, and the Fair Gwen grabs Freak and puts him in the wagon and I swear, she almost *runs* home, like if she doesn't get away quickly something really bad is going to happen. Freak is in the wagon and he's trying to look back at me, trying to shrug his shoulders and let me know he doesn't understand what got into the Fair Gwen, but *I* know.

It's pretty simple, really. She's scared of me.

# Spitting Image 5

There's a place I go inside my head sometimes. It's cool and dim in there and you float like a cloud – no, you *are* a cloud, the kind you see in the sky on a windy day, the way they keep changing shape except you can't really *see* it changing? It just sort of happens, and suddenly you realize the cloud that looks like a big hand with fat fingers now looks like a catcher's mitt, or a big soft TV set? Like that.

Anyhow, I went there right after the Fair Gwen ran off with that look on her face, like: What was he *doing* with my poor little boy, stealing him away in the wagon?

What I do is lie on the floor under my bed, where you can just barely see the bedsprings and stuff because it's so dark, and before long I'm somewhere else, sort of floating, and it's so cool and empty on there, you don't have to think about anything. You're nothing, you're nobody, nothing matters, you're not even there. *Time out.*

Except this time I can't stay as long as I'd like because Gram is knocking on the door. Going, "Maxwell? Max, are you there? Please answer me, dear, it's important."

Yeah, right. But I wedge out from under the bed – there's getting to be less and less room under there – and I dust myself off and open the door. There's no lock, but Gram has this thing about waiting until I say come in, she makes a big deal about not intruding.

"Maxwell," she says, and she takes a little step inside the room and you can tell she'd rather not be here, she makes this face because the place is dark and messy and probably it smells like my socks or whatever. "Max, dear, I'm sorry to bother you – you know I *never* come into the basement – but I just got a call from Gwen Avery and I thinks it's important."

Uh-oh, I'm thinking. Now the Fair Gwen is calling up my Gram, probably to report a great hulking beast that lives in the cellar, and I close up inside, waiting for the worst.

"She called to say how sorry she was," Gram is saying.

"Huh?"

"I guess she came to pick up her little boy, is that right? You and Kevin were making friends?"

*Making friends*. What a wet idea *that* is, but Gram gets her feelings hurt pretty easy, so I don't actually say that. What I say is, "Yeah, I guess so."

Gram is uneasy, I can see her eyes flitting nervously around the room, like she's crossing the border into a really foreign country. This is as good a place as any to mention that even though Gram is my grandmother, she doesn't *look* like a granny, she looks more like a mother because she was, as she always says, "a mere child myself" when my real mother was born.

"Well, uhm, I get the impression poor Gwen wasn't expecting to see you looking so big, and now she thinks she's offended you. Does that make any sense?"

"I guess so. You know her, huh?"

"Oh my yes," says Gram. "Gwen was a good friend of your mother's. They were both pregnant at the same time. Then later on you and little Kevin went to the same day care, did you know that?"

I give a shrug because I don't really like Gram to know how much I remember about way back then.

Gram is saying, "She said – she especially wanted

me to tell you this, Max – she said she's delighted that you and Kevin are going to be friends. That's the word she used – delighted. And she's invited you to supper."

First thing, without thinking, I say, "Do I have to?"

Gram reaches out and puts her hand on my shoulder, real light and feathery, you can feel how nervous she is just to touch me, and how it makes her uncomfortable to have to look up to me, because did I mention I'm a lot bigger than Gram? Bigger than Grim, too? Bigger than most people? It's true.

Gram says, "She feels bad about how she treated you, Maxwell, dear, and she wants to make it up to you. You don't *have* to go, but it would be the right thing to do."

"It was no big deal," I say. "She just ran away is all. I guess I scared her."

"It wasn't you," Gram says.

"No? Then who was it scared her?"

Now she's got her tongue stuck, and you can see her swallowing in her throat, like her mouth is dry. "I'll just leave that to Gwen," she says. "She's quite a remarkable woman, you know. Raising that poor boy all on her own."

"He's not a poor boy," I say. "You should hear

him talk. I think the rest of him is so small because his brain is so big."

"Yes," says Gram. "Well well."

Gram is always saying that, well well, like it means something, which I guess it does to her. Anyhow, I agree to have supper with Freak and his mom, even though the idea of it makes me feel tensed up, like there is a hand inside my stomach and the hand is, you know, making a fist.

* * *

It turns out to be not so bad. The Fair Gwen, right away she's beaming at me, bouncing around the kitchen and talking a mile a minute, so fast the words kind of smoosh together.

"SodidSusanexcusemeyourgrandmothermention yourmomandIwerepalsthatis...untilshegotmarried excusemeInever...*could*abidethatmanIalwaysthoughthe wascrazyand...scaryisitokaytosaythatyou...won'tbe offended?"

It's like this delay while I sort it out, and then I go, "Yeah, Gram told me," and the stuff about her knowing my father and thinking he was sick in the head, I decide no comment is the way to go.

"You were the cutest little baby," Gwen says. "I

remember like it was yesterday. We were all of us living over in the tenements in those days, because the rent was so cheap and we were all just starting out."

Freak is on the floor, digging through the packing boxes for pots and pans and stuff, he's almost inside this box, all you can see is his funny little rear end sticking out. You'd think he was maybe two years old, that's how small he is, until you notice where his leg brace makes a lump in his pants.

From inside the box he goes, "Hey, Gwen, leave the guy alone, huh? You're going spastic."

"Am I?" Gwen asks. She's at the counter, going through drawers and looking for spoons or whatever. "Sorry, Max. That is, I'm sorry we got off on the wrong foot. It's just, you know. . ."

Freak's head pops out of the box and he's got this wicked know-it-all grin. "What she means is, you're the spitting image of your old man."

Gwen says, "Kevin, please," and her voice is real small, like she's embarrassed.

"Yeah," I say. "Everybody says that."

"They do?"

I shrug. Is it really such a big deal for a boy to look like his father? Which is typical butthead thinking, because of course it's a big deal, if your father happens to be in prison. Which everybody in town knows about, it's not like there's any secret about what he did or why he's there, except everybody *acts* like it should be a secret, and the bigger I grow and the more I look like my old man, the worse it gets.

"You really knew him?" I say. "I mean him and my mom when they were together?"

"Not very well," Gwen says. She's looking for a knife to slice open a pack of hot dogs. "I never saw much of your mom after they got married. He made it. . .difficult for your mother to have any friends."

There's a knife on the table and I pick it up and hand it to the Fair Gwen. She doesn't really flinch away and I decide she's okay, she's really pretty cool.

"So," Freak is saying. "When do we eat? My fuel cells are depleted."

* * *

Supper is great. The Fair Gwen makes this really tasty potato salad with spices and stuff, way better than the mushy stuff Gram makes, and we have hot dogs fried in a pan with the buns toasted up butter-crisp just the way I like, and two kinds of relish and three kinds of mustard, and red onions cut up real small.

We sit out in the back yard eating from paper

plates, and Freak tells robot stories that are so strange and funny I'm laughing like a maniac and then I'm choking and Freak is pounding me on the back.

"Expel the object!" Freak shouts. "Regurgitate, you big moron!" and he gives me another thump and I cough up this yucky mess, but I'm still laughing so hard my nose is running.

What a goon, except it really *is* funny, me trying to sneeze a hot dog through my nose, and we're both laughing like total morons.

"This is great," Gwen says, looking at Freak and me. "I'm glad we decided to move back, you know? I feel like we're all getting a fresh start."

It's time to go home, Gram gets nervous if I'm not back before dark. Everything seems really great, just like Gwen says, except when I lie down on my bed it hits me, boom, and I'm crying like a baby. And the really weird thing is, I'm happy.

# Close Encounter 6 of the Turd Kind

Fourth of July, right? Everybody goes nuts. The dads are getting drunk and having their cookouts, and the moms are trying to keep all the brats from blowing their precious little pinkies off with cherry bombs, and the kids are running wild through the back yards. It's like no rules apply, and that makes everything real *edgy*, if you know what I mean, like let's have a blast and who cares what happens.

Don't get the wrong idea. I *love* the Fourth. It's just that people tend to get all choked up about firecracker holidays, and they don't see what's *really* going on, which like I say is the dads swilling beer and acting numb, that's the basic formula.

Not that Grim ever swills anything stronger than root beer. No way. The poison never crossed his lips, he likes to say, even though I've seen a picture of him in the army and that sure *looks* like a bottle of beer in his hand, and he's got that same wacked-by-a-hammer grin that dudes always get when they're drinking.

Anyhow, this is the first year I get to go to the fireworks without Grim and Gram, which I've never understood, because it's right down by the millpond where I've been allowed to go for years, so why should it make a difference just because about a million people show up to watch the rockets' red glare over that smelly pond?

The deal this year is that I get to go with Freak, which Gram thinks is a good idea because she's afraid he'll get crushed or something, she actually thinks people are going to *step* on him, which just goes to show how brainless she can be sometimes, and scared of everything. I mean nobody steps on little kids down there, so why should they step on Freak?

Turns out the thing to worry about is not kidstompers, but beer swillers, like I mentioned before. Because Freak and I are still a couple of blocks from the pond, just kind of easing our way along, when these punks start mouthing off.

"Hey you! Mutt and Jeff! Frankenstein and Igor! Don't look around, I'm talkin' to you, boneheads. What is this, a freak show?"

I know that voice. Tony D., they call him Blade, he's at least seventeen and he's already been to juvy court three, four times. I heard he cut a guy with a razor, and he almost died, and everybody says the best way to handle Tony D. and his gang is, you avoid them. Cross the street, hide, whatever it takes.

"Yeah you," he goes, and he's doing his hippity walk, strutting along, he's got these fancy cool cowboy boots with metal toes. "Yeah, Andre the Giant and the dwarf, hold on a sec, I want a word with you."

Only the way he talks, he goes ah wanna woid weecha, except it's bad enough having to listen to the creep, I don't want to have to spell the dumb way he talks. Anyhow, big mistake, we stop and wait for Tony D., alias the bad-news Blade.

"Got any, dudes?" he asks, pretending like he's friendly. He's a couple feet away, but you can smell the beer on his breath. Also it smells like he ate something dead, for instance road kill, but maybe that's my imagination.

"Pay attention," Tony D. says. "I asked did you got any."

Freak, his chest is all puffed out and his chin looks hard and he's looking right up at Tony D., and he says, "Got any what?"

Tony D. has his hands on his hips and his punkster pals are trying to get closer, working through the crowd. He leans over Freak and he says, "Boomers, you little freak. M80s. Maybe a rack of cherry bombs, is that what's making a lump in your pocket, huh?"

Freak starts to hump himself away, trying to walk faster than he can, which makes his leg brace bump against the ground. "Come along, Maxwell," he says over his shoulder. "Ignore the cretin."

Blade goes, "Hey what?" and he moves right in front of Freak. "Want to say that again, little freak man?"

Freak says, "Cretin. C-R-E-T-I-N. Defined as one who suffers from mental deficiency."

Hearing how little tiny Freak is dissing the fearsome Tony D., alias Blade, I can't help it, I laugh out loud. Tony D. is looking up at me and he's showing his white teeth, I swear they've been sharpened to look like vampire teeth, and I go, "Uh-oh," and start to get real cold inside. Real icy, because I can see that Blade is trying to make up his mind, is he going to fight me, or is he just going to kill me quick?

Just then I hear the whoop of a siren and like a miracle this cop car comes out of nowhere, heading for the millpond, and Blade takes one look and he and his punksters are out of there, burning rubber in their Reeboks.

Freak goes, "Whew! That was a close encounter of the turd kind," and it takes me a second to get the joke, but then I'm laughing, amazed he can be so cool about it, like it was no big deal that Tony D. was after us.

"You *can* take him, right?" he asks a couple minutes later.

I go, "Are you kidding? You can't just fight Blade, you have to fight his gang, too."

"You mean you *couldn't* take him and I was giving him lip?"

"That's about the size of it."

Freak goes, "Oh my *gawwwwwwd!*" and he's shrieking and laughing and whooping it up so loud that everybody is looking at us like we're total goons, which isn't far from the truth.

Freak hasn't got his crutch tonight, just the leg brace, and he's laughing so hard he falls down. Not that he has far to go. Anyhow, I pick him up and I'm amazed at how light he is. Like it's *nothing* for me to lift him, and maybe that's where I get the idea. Because later, when we're down by the pond and the first of the rockets is streaking up, up, up, Freak is making a fuss because he can't see. There are so many people crowded around, all he can see are feet and knees, and people are lifting their little kids up to see the fireworks explode like hot pink flowers in the sky, and so I just sort of reach down without thinking and pick up Freak and set him on my shoulders.

He's kind of trembly up there until he grabs hold of my hair to steady himself, and then the first really big rocket whams off, a humongous *thud*! I can feel in my stomach, and Freak is shouting, "Awwww *right*!" and I know it's okay, he's not flipped out because I picked him up and put him on my shoulders like he was a little kid instead of possibly the smartest human being in the whole world.

"Magnesium!" he shouts as the white sparkles glitter down over the pond. "Potassium chlorate!" as the shells go womp-womp-womp and everybody goes oooooooh. "Potassium nitrate! Sulphur! Aluminium!" And after a burst of hot red fire in the sky, Freak tugs my hair and screams, "Copper! That's copper powder combusting with oxygen!" And when the fire blossoms are flashing blue he goes, "Good old strontium nitrate!" and I'm thinking whoa! is there anything this little dude *doesn't* know?

36

At the end, like always, they have a thing they call the "grand finale", when they just go nuts and light off everything at once and it sounds like World War III, whizzing and banging and popping, and there's so much hot stuff falling from the sky you can hear it sizzling in the pond. Freak keeps on shouting out the names of chemicals and elements, until the last spark dies in that scummy pond and the crowd cheers and then everybody tries to leave at once, like a bunch of morons.

# 7 Walking High
## Above the World

You ever notice how the smell of gunpowder makes you thirsty? Because after the fireworks I'm aiming us for where the food carts are parked along the street, thinking about an ice-cold lemonade, how *clean* it will taste, and for a moment I almost forget that Freak is riding on my shoulders.

"Amazing perspective up here," he's saying. "This is what you see all the time."

"I'm not *that* big," I say. "This way you're like two feet taller than me."

"Cool," he says. "I love it."

We're working our way through the crowd and we're almost to the food carts when Freak tugs on my hair. "Cretin at two o'clock," he says, real urgent. "Two more at three o'clock."

I go, "Huh? What?"

"The Blade and his gang," Freak hisses. "They've locked on to us. Their trajectory is converging. Go to the left," he says. "Make it quick, if you want to live!"

Too bad I'm a little confused about rights and lefts. If I don't think about it I know, but if I have to think about it quick my mind goes blank. Right? Left? What does it all *mean*?

"Left!" Freak says, and he kicks me with his little foot, like he's digging into a horse and it clicks in my head. Go that way! Follow the feet! "Faster," Freak is saying, and he's urging me on, it's lucky for me the little dude doesn't have any spurs, but I don't care, I just want to get clear of Blade.

"Warp factor nine!" Freak is shouting. "More speed, o mighty beast!"

Now I'm running at a full gallop, weaving through the crowd, and I don't even need to look back, all I have to do is follow the way Freak is kicking his feet, steering me. I'm pretty sure we're getting away until this punk comes out of nowhere, he's one of Blade's gang and he's got this big ugly grin.

"Over here! Tony! Got 'em cornered!"

"What do I do?" I say to Freak.

He goes, "I'm thinking, I'm thinking!"

I can hear Blade before I can see him. Hear his wicked laugh, so mean and dirty it makes my stomach freeze up and my knees feel squishy.

"You! The freak! You and that giant retard, I'll cut you down to size. Dice and slice, baby! Freak show time!"

And now I can see him, see that pointed white grin and his eyes so dark and cruel, and he's swaggering through the crowd, he's got us surrounded with punks, everywhere I turn there's another mean face trying to look as tough as Tony D.

In a small voice I say, "Tell me what to do," and Freak pats me on the shoulder and says, "Just give me a nanosecond to process the alternatives."

"Slice and dice!" That's Blade, and he's reaching into his back pocket.

"Make it quick," I hiss, and then Freak is kicking my right shoulder and I turn that way and he's saying, "Go! Go!" and I run right over this punk, he's so surprised he loses his bubble gum and he tries to grab my leg but I kick free and I'm running right and then left, running blind and just letting Freak decide which way we should go because he must have a plan, a dude as smart as that.

Which I'm right about, he *does* have a plan. Only the plan is to run out into the smelly millpond and drown us both.

"Go on!" he's shouting from up above my head.

"Trust me, we'll be okay!"

Blade is shouting too, and I can hear his feet pitter-pattering behind me. Catching up.

"Warp speed!" Freak is shouting, and he's kicking with both feet now, which means go straight. "Head for the $H_2O$!"

The pond is right ahead of me, and I'm sort of running along the edge, crunching over the bottles and cans and candy wrappers, and then I hear this zingy sound and I just know that Blade is swinging a knife, cutting the air right behind us, and there's nowhere to go but into the pond, like Freak wants me to.

I almost lose it right there, taking that first step, because it's a gunky pond and the mud is really oozy and deep and it sucks right up to my knees. But I'm so scared of getting cut by Tony D., so scared he might *bite* me with those wicked teeth, I just keep going. There's this great ugly *sucking* sound as my feet come back up out of the mud and I stretch out as far as my legs will go and I take another step and I just keep going.

I'm going so fast that the water is up to my chest before Freak gets my attention, he's tugging at my hair with both hands. "Whoa!" he's saying, "slow up, we did it."

41

The mud is up around my knees and it's real hard to turn around. Finally I get so I'm facing back at the shore and there's Blade, just his head above the water, and he looks all white and scared. "Help!" he's blubbering, choking on that dirty water, and then his punksters are splashing in to rescue him. Man, they can hardly get him loose, the way he's stuck deep in that mud, and before they drag him to shore they're all covered with slime and mud. They're gasping like fish, almost too tired to cuss us out, but that doesn't last.

Blade is covered with mud right up to his neck, which on him looks natural. He turns to his gang, who look as slimy as he does. "Get some rocks, it's target-practice time!"

"What do we do now?" I ask, because the mud is still sucking me down. It's over my knees now, and the water is right up under my arms and even Freak's feet are getting wet.

"Wait," Freak says. "The cavalry is coming, can't you hear that bugle?"

I'm listening, but I can't hear anything except for Blade and his gang, and how they're scrambling around trying to find some rocks to heave at us.

I can see Blade rearing back to throw, and the first one misses us.

"Can you move?" Freak says.

"I don't think so."

It's true. The mud is up over my knees, and I'm locked in place. I can't even fall down, that's how stiff it is. I'm like a big fence post, and everybody knows a fence post makes a good target.

More splashes as the rocks fall short. At first they're throwing stuff that's too heavy. Pretty soon they smarten up, and Blade says, "Smaller rocks! Get me smaller rocks!" and I know in my heart we're doomed.

Then up above me there's this really loud, high-pitched screech. Freak has his fingers in his mouth and he's whistling. Real shrill and shivery and so loud it almost hurts my ears. And then I see what Freak has been seeing all along, a cop car cruising real slow along the road around the pond, which is what they always do after the fireworks.

Freak is whistling and the cop car spotlight comes beaming around the pond until it settles on us. I'm blinking because the light is so bright, and Freak is making a fuss and waving his arms and we hear the metal megaphone sound of a cop voice ordering us not to move. Like we could even if we wanted!

It's hard to see in the glare of the spotlight, but

Freak tells me that Blade and his punks are running away. Like snakes on sneakers, Freak says.

"Officers!" Freak is shouting into the white light. "We request assistance!"

They finally have to use ropes to pull me out of there. Freak won't let go, he stays right where he is on top of my shoulders even when this cop in a boat tries to lift him off, and then we're up on the bank of the pond and everybody is being real nice and giving us blankets and Cokes and saying they know all about Tony D., they'll keep an eye on him, don't you worry.

"Okay, boys, you'd better give us your names and we'll call your mothers," this one cop is saying, and there's this other guy who is looking at me funny and he says, "Hey, isn't that Kenny Kane's boy? Must be. Old Killer Kane, is he still inside?"

Freak is still holding tight to my shoulders and when they ask him for his name, he says, "We're Freak the Mighty, that's who we are. We're nine feet tall, in case you haven't noticed."

That's how it started, really, how we got to be Freak the Mighty, slaying dragons and fools and walking high above the world.

# Dinosaur Brain 8

It turned out to be a cool summer.

I figured we'd get into trouble for running into the pond. It looked bad for a while when the cops drove us home and I got out all soaking wet and covered with gook, and when Grim was hosing me down he had this really pruney look on his face, like he was smelling something bad, but the cops made out like I was a hero or something, rescuing the poor crippled midget kid. So Grim listens to the cops and then he gives me this weird look, like, *imagine my surprise*, and he goes into the house and then Gram comes running out in her nightgown with this big fluffy towel and she really makes a fuss.

Me rescuing Freak. What a joke, right? Except that's how it must have looked from a distance because they never knew it was Freak who rescued me – or his genius brain and my big dumb body.

Gram is there rubbing me with the towel and her hands are shaking and she's saying, "Oh, I saw those blue lights and I thought the worst," and Grim is behind her looking at me real intense and shaking his head, and he's saying, "Who'd a thunk it, Mabel," which is some kind of joke because Gram's name isn't Mabel.

Anyhow, they take me inside and the first thing Gram does is give me a bowl of ice cream, and Grim, he keeps shaking his head and he goes, "What this young man needs is a cup of coffee. Real coffee," and then he gets busy putting the filter in the machine and measuring out the coffee and standing by while it drips through, and he's got this stern look like he's thinking deep thoughts. By the time I polish off the ice cream, Grim is handing me coffee in a china cup, from the set they never use.

He gives me the cup like it's a really big deal, maybe because I'm not allowed to drink coffee yet, and he's so Grim-like and serious I open my mouth to say what's the big deal, you really think this is my first cup of coffee (yeah, right!), and something happens and the words come out: "Thank you, sir," and it's like I'm *possessed* or something, I've no idea where the things I'm saying are coming from, or why.

I go, "Thanks for the towel, Gram. And the ice cream. Could I have sugar in the coffee? Two teaspoons, please," and Grim claps his hands together and he says, "Of course you can, son," and it's like *whoa!* because he never calls me that. Always Max or Maxwell or "that boy".

Next thing he's clearing his throat and coughing into his fist and Gram is looking at the two of us and she gets this Gram-like glow, like this is how it's *supposed* to be, the way things always happen on *The Wonder Years*, with the family getting all gooey and sentimental about some numb thing the bratty kid did while he's having all his wonderful years or whatever.

Gram says, "I want you to promise me something, Maxwell dear. Promise me you'll keep away from that hoodlum boy and his awful friends. Nobody got hurt this time, but I shudder to think what *might* have happened."

And Grim, bless his pointed little head, he goes, "Maxwell can handle himself, can't you, uh, Max?"

Right. *Uh, Max.* Not son. Which is okay by me.

"I can run," I say to Gram. "I see Tony D., that's what I'll do."

"Good boy," Gram says. "I thought, because you're so much bigger than he is. . .well, you just do that, dear. You run away."

"He's not running away," Grim says, real impatient. "He's taking evasive action. Avoiding a confrontation. That's a very different thing, right, Max?"

I nod and drink my coffee without slurping and decide it's better not to mention that Tony D. carries a knife and he's probably got guns, too, because then Gram would only worry and she's such a clunker when she's worried.

\* \* \*

Like I said, it turns out to be a pretty cool summer. Usually what I do is hang around and look at my comic books and watch the tube, or go shopping with Gram if she really makes a fuss. I hate the beach because the beach is stupid, the cool crowd looking sleek and tanned and aren't-we-gorgeous?, and because if you saw me lying on a blanket you'd go, hey, why is that albino walrus wearing sunglasses?

So mostly I just vegetate in the basement and pick my navel, to quote Grim, Mr. Belly Button Lint himself.

Freak changes all that. Each and every morning the little dude humps himself over and he bangs on the bulkhead, wonka-wonka-wonka, he may be small but he sure is noisy. "Get outta bed, you lazy beast! There are fair maidens to rescue! Dragons to slay!" which is what he says every single morning, exactly the same thing, until it's like he's this alarm clock and as soon as I hear the wonka-wonka-wonka of him beating the bulkhead, I know what's coming next: fair maidens and dragons, and Freak with that wake-up-the-world grin of his, going, "Hurry up with the cereal, how can you eat that much, you big ox, come on, let's *do* something," he's so full of eveready energy you can practically hear his brain humming, and he can never sit still.

"Ants in the pants," I say one morning when he's ready to yank the cereal bowl off the table, he's in such a hurry to *do* something, and he goes, "What?" and I go, "You must have ants in your pants," and he gets this funny look and he goes, "That's what the Fair Gwen always says, did she tell you to say that?" and I shake my head and finish the cereal real slow and Freak goes, "For your information there are two thousand two hundred and forty-seven known subspecies of hymenopteran insects, Latin name *Formicidae*, and *none* of them are in my pants."

Which cracks me up, even though I don't understand a word he's saying.

"I propose a quest," he says. "We shall journey far to the East and see what lies there."

By now I know what a quest is because Freak has explained the whole deal, how it started with King Arthur trying to keep all his knights busy by making them do things that proved how strong and brave and smart they were, or sometimes how totally numb, because how else can you explain dudes running around inside big clunky tin cans and praying all the time? Which I don't mention to Freak because he's very sensitive about knights and quests and secret meanings. Like how a dragon isn't really just a big slimy fire-breathing monster, it's a symbol of nature or something.

"A dragon is fear of the natural world," Freak says. "An archetype of the unknown."

I go, "What's an archy-type?" and Freak sighs and shakes his head and reaches into his knapsack for his dictionary.

This is true. He really *does* keep a dictionary in his knapsack, it's his favourite book, and he pulls it out like Arnold Schwarzenegger pulling out a machine gun or something, that's the fierce look he gets with a book in his hands.

"Go on," he says, making me take the book, "look it up." And now I wish I hadn't said anything about this archetype dude because I *hate* looking up stuff in his stupid dictionary.

"Start with A," he says.

"I know that."

"A-R," he says. "Just go along the A's until you come to A-R."

Yeah, right. Easy for a genius to use the dictionary, since he already knows how to spell the words. And R's never look like backward E's to Freak, which is the way they look to me sometimes, unless I really squint and think about it.

"Careful," he says. "You'll bite off your tongue and then we'll have to waste the day at the emergency room, getting it reattached. Microsurgery is *such* a bore, didn't anybody ever tell you that?"

"Huh?" I say, but I do close my mouth so my tongue doesn't stick out. I'm still looking in the dictionary for "archetype" and I'm looking for words that are underlined in red ink, because that's what Freak does the first time he looks up a word, he makes a line under it, and you'd be amazed how many are underlined, there are whole *pages* like that, where he's looked up every single word.

Finally he spells out all the letters for me, and I find the stupid word.

"There's nothing about dragons here," I say, squinting hard at the stuff under the word. "It just says 'pattern'. So what is it, a sewing type of thing?"

Freak has this disgusted look and he takes the dictionary and he goes, "You're hopeless. Pattern is the first definition. I was referring to the *second* definition, which is more interesting. 'A universal symbol or idea in the psyche, expressed in dreams or dreamlike images'."

Like that helps, right? I'm getting bored with the dictionary, so I pretend to understand and Freak finally gives up and he shakes his head and goes, "I don't know why I bother. Dinosaurs had brains the size of peanuts and they ruled the earth for a hundred million years."

# Life Is Dangerous 9

So out we go. It's a habit by now, Freak riding up high on my shoulders and using his little feet to steer me if I forget where we're going. Not that we always know. Freak likes to make things up as he goes along. You think you're just walking down this ordinary sidewalk and really you're crossing this dangerous bridge, the kind made of vines that hangs high up in the air over a deep canyon, and when Freak makes it up it seems so real, you're afraid to look down or you'll get dizzy and fall off the sidewalk.

"Don't ever look down," he says. "Just keep your eyes closed." And then he puts his hands over my eyes and tells me to keep walking straight. "One foot," he says. "Now the next."

I'm fighting to keep my balance, and his hands are making me dizzy.

"One more step," Freak says. "Steady. Steady. Now lift up your hoof – I mean your foot. There, we made it!" And he takes his hands away and I see we've crossed the street.

"Go East," he says when I get to the end of the block. "That way, mighty steed! Yonder lies the East!"

I go, "How do you know which way is East?" And then something is glinting in my eye and Freak is showing me this little compass.

"The Official Cub Scout Compass?"

"That's a clever disguise so you don't know how valuable it is," he says. "This is actually a rare and valuable artifact passed down for generations. Lancelot used it, so did Sir Gawain, and for a time the Black Knight kept it on a chain next to his heart."

I go, "So the Black Knight was a Cub Scout, huh?" and Freak laughs and says, "That way. We go to the East on a secret mission."

We walk for miles. Way beyond the pond and the playground and the school, and for a while we're going through this really ritzy neighbourhood of big white houses and blue swimming pools. Freak keeps saying stuff like, "That's the Castle of Avarice," and, "Yonder lies the Bloated Moat," and when we go under trees he'll say, "Proceed with caution," or, "All clear," depending on how low the branches come down.

"We must be East," I say. "Have we got to yonder yet?" because my stupid feet are getting sore, but Freak pats me on the head and says, "Yonder always lies over the horizon. You could look it up if you don't believe me."

"Oh, I believe you."

On and on, block after block, through all these neighbourhoods that Freak says are really secret kingdoms. I'll bet we've gone ten miles at least, because my legs think it's a hundred, and even as light as Freak is, he's starting to feel heavy.

"We're almost there," he says. "Turn at the end of the block."

"Where is it we're going?"

"You'll see," he says, "and you *will* be amazed."

Ahead there's this busy intersection, cars whizzing by, and it all seems sort of familiar.

"Can we stop for a Coke?" I say. "Grim gave me a dollar, big deal, but we can split it."

Freak goes, "Then that shall be your reward, faithful steed – tinted sucrose and bubbles of air. Onward! Onward to the Fortress!"

It turns out the Fortress looks like part of a hospital, which it is. The regular hospital is around the front and there's this new building added on out back. MEDICAL RESEARCH, it says over the door, and I know because I made Freak spell it out.

"Does that mean they do experiments and stuff?"

Freak says, "Indeed they do."

"What kind of experiments?" I ask.

"Can you keep a secret?" he says. "Do you swear on your honour?"

"Sure. On my honour."

Freak is really excited, he's shifting around on my shoulders so much, I'm afraid he'll fall off. "That's not good enough," he says. "You need to swear by your blood."

"You mean like cut myself?"

"Well, no," he says, and you can tell he's thinking about it real hard. "An actual incision is not necessary. It's the same thing if you just spit on your hand."

"Huh?"

"Saliva is like blood without the red," he says. "Do as I say, spit in your hand."

So I spit in my hand, just a little drop, but Freak says it doesn't matter how much, a single molecule would work, because it's the principle of the thing. "Now put your hand over your heart," he says.

I put my hand over my heart.

"Now swear on your heart that the data you are

about to receive will be divulged to no one."

"I swear."

Freak bends down and he's got his hand cupped around my ear and he's whispering: "Inside the research building is a secret laboratory called The Experimental Bionics Unit. The unit's mission is to develop a new form of bionic robot for human modification."

"What's that?" I say.

"Shhh! Speak of this to no one, but at some future time as yet undetermined, I will enter that lab and become the first bionically improved human."

"I still don't know what it means," I say. "Bionics. And please don't make me look it up in the dictionary."

"Bionics," Freak says. "That's the science of designing replacement parts for the human body."

"You mean like mechanical arms and legs?"

"That's ancient history," Freak says. "The Bionics Unit is building a whole new body just my size."

"Yeah? What'll it look like? A robot?"

"A human robot," Freak says. "Also it will look a lot like me, only enlarged and improved."

"Yeah, right," I say. "Let's go home, my feet are tired."

Freak tugs hard at my hair. "True!" he says, with

his voice getting high and excited. "I've been in there, in the special unit! I have to go every few months for tests. They've taken my measurements, analysed my blood and metabolic rates. They've monitored my cardiac rhythms and my respiratory functions. I've already been X-rayed and CAT-scanned and sonogrammed. They're fitting me for a bionic transplant, I'm going to be the first."

I can tell he really means it. This isn't a pretend quest, or making houses into castles or swimming pools into moats. This is why we came here, so Freak could show me where he's been. The place is important to him. I understand this much, even if I still don't understand about bionics or what it means to be a human robot.

"Will it hurt?" I ask. "Getting your parts replaced?"

Freak doesn't answer for a while and then he says in his stern, smart voice, "Sure it will hurt. But so what? Pain is just a state of mind. You can think your way out of anything, even pain."

I'm pretty worried about the whole deal, and I go, "But why do you want to be the first? Can't someone else be first? Isn't it dangerous?"

"Life is dangerous," Freak says, and you can tell he's thought a lot about this. After a while he kicks me with his little feet and says, "Home."

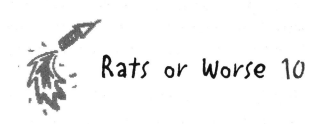

# Rats or Worse 10

One thing that happened over the summer, I grew even more.

Grim takes a look at me one day and he goes, "All that walking you do, it must be stretching out your legs. And carrying poor Kevin around, that seems to be putting real muscle on you."

"He's not that heavy. And anyhow it's not fair everybody always says 'Poor Kevin,' just because he didn't grow."

Grim gives me this long, sorrowful look and then he clears his throat and says, "You're quite right, he *is* a rather remarkable boy."

"He's memorized almost the whole dictionary. You can ask him anything and he knows what it means."

"You don't say," Grim says, and he has this smug

look like maybe Freak is lying and a total goon like me would never get it, and I want to tell him he's wrong about Freak and the dictionary, but instead I just shut my face and go down under.

Grim, he's okay sometimes, like when Tony D. chased us into the pond, but most of the time he thinks he knows everything, which he doesn't. And if you don't believe me, look under "grim" in the dictionary, it sure doesn't say "a smart grown-up". No way.

So I'm hanging out down under, listening to some of my thrash tapes on the fake Walkman I got last Christmas, when Freak pops up on the side of my bed. Because of the headphones and the volume being pumped up to mega-decibel I never hear him come in, he's just suddenly *there*, like whoa! and I'll bet I jumped about a foot.

Freak rolls his eyes and goes, "Ah, music, how it calms the savage beast."

"How'd you get here?"

"Would you believe teleportation? No? Then I came down through the bulkhead door like always. And like always, I have a quest in mind."

Right away I go, "My feet hurt."

"We don't have to leave this neighbourhood."

"Cool. What kind of quest is this?"

Freak grins. "A treasure hunt. Except we don't really have to hunt because I already know where the treasure is."

"Where?"

"Underground," he says. "Specifically, in the sewer."

"Yeah, right," I say and sit back down on the bed. Freak is looking at me sideways and I can tell he's not telling me everything, which he almost never does, not all at once.

"Truth," he says. "The treasure is hidden in a storm drain. This has been confirmed by visual observation."

"Treasure in a storm drain? You mean like gold and diamonds kind of stuff?"

"Possibly," he says, acting mysterious. "Anything is possible."

The deal is, we have to wait until night, so no one can see us messing with the storm drain. Not just night, Freak says, we need to do it at exactly three in the morning.

"Optimum darkness occurs at oh-three-hundred hours," he says, looking at the new watch his mom gave him, the kind that tells you what time it is in Tokyo, just in case you're wondering. "We must dress in black and cover our faces with soot."

For the next couple of hours we try to find soot, but it turns out you need a fireplace for soot, or at least a chimney, so Freak finally decides that my idea about using regular dirt will have to do.

"I've got black dungarees," I say, "but no black shirts. Can I just wear a dirty shirt?"

Freak makes a face and says, "What a *disgusting* idea. Don't worry about the shirt, I'll get you one. Can you manage black socks?"

* * *

You ever notice how long it takes for things to happen when you know they're *supposed* to happen? My fake Walkman has a built-in alarm, and I set it for two in the morning and wear the headphones to bed, but before you can wake up you have to fall asleep, and I never *do* fall asleep because I keep waiting for the alarm to go off. Which is, I know, typical butthead behaviour.

I'm lying awake in the dark on a hot summer night and I'm thinking, *Treasure in the sewer? What kind of quest is this, huh? Is Freak completely making this up or what?*

Meanwhile there's this cricket making this creaky cricket noise that normally is okay, except when you're trying to fall asleep then it's *not* okay, and you want a big can of Raid, send it to Disney World or insect heaven or wherever it is that dead crickets go.

Question: How come Freak knows about this stuff in the storm drain?

Question: How come we have to put dirt on our faces?

Question: How come three in the morning?

Question: How long do crickets live?

Finally I give up on the first three and work on the cricket problem, but the little critter is pretty clever, it stops cricketing whenever I get too close, and I never *do* find it and squash it with my shoe, which I swear I am ready to do, even if crickets are supposed to be harmless.

And then after almost for ever it gets to be two-thirty and I figure that's close enough, I'll go up and wait under Freak's window like I promised.

There's no moon, the sky is dark and empty, and the back yards are so lonesome it feels creepy and exciting – the truth is, I've never been out alone at this time of night.

I only fall down a couple of times, which isn't bad considering how hard it is to see. When I get to Freak's bedroom window, he's waiting for me.

"You sound like a car wreck," he says. "Here,

you better put on this shirt so you don't glow in the dark."

Out of the window he hands me this silly-feeling shirt.

"Hey wait a minute, this is your mom's blouse!"

"It's black," he says. "That's what counts. The camouflage factor."

"Forget it," I say and give him back the Fair Gwen's blouse.

Freak sighs. "Okay," he says. "Roll around on the ground and darken yourself."

That's easy, and better than wearing some dumb blouse. "What about you?" I ask, when I'm covered with dirt, enough so I want to sneeze.

Freak goes, "Beware the Force, earthling," and he stands up in the window and I can see he's got a Darth Vader costume on, except he's not wearing the mask part. He opens the window all the way and I lift him out and put him on my shoulders.

He goes, "Pledge to me your fealty," and I say, "Huh?" and he says, "Never mind, there's no time to look up 'fealty'. Just promise you'll do what I say."

"I promise."

"Go to the end of the block," he orders. "Attempt to conceal us in the shadows."

That's easy, because the street is one big shadow. It's so dark I can hardly see my feet, or maybe I got some dirt in my eyes, but the point is no one sees us because there's no one to see us. You'd never know anybody lived here, let alone a whole blockful of people, it's like we're on an empty planet or something.

"Was the real Darth Vader as tall as this?" Freak asks from where he's riding high up on my shoulders.

"I thought it was just a movie."

"You know what I mean. What's that!"

"That" is a cat that runs out from under my feet so out-of-nowhere sudden that my heart goes *wham*.

"Was it a black cat?" Freak wants to know.

"Too dark to tell," I say. "Are we almost there?"

Finally I figure out it's hard to see because the Darth Vader cape is hanging in my eyes, but by then we're at the end of the block and the storm drain is right there by the kerb.

"See if you can pull it open," Freak says. He's standing with his arms folded, and the expression on his face – well, he really *does* look like a pint-sized Darth Vader.

I hook my hands in the storm drain grate and give it a heave but nothing happens.

"I can't budge it."

"Try again," he says with his arms folded, like he's a lord of the universe.

I try again and it's like the grate is Super Glued or something. No way can I pull it up. Freak is tugging at my leg and he goes, "Option Two is now in effect."

He reaches inside his little cape. Out comes a flashlight, one of those small kinds that look sort of like a cigarette lighter, and also a spool of kite string.

"I devised a special retrieval device," Freak says.

"Looks like a bent paper clip on a string," I say, and Freak tells me to shut up and follow orders.

"You hold the string," he says, and then he gets down on his knees and shines the little flashlight through the grate. "Can you see it?" he asks. "Can you?"

I look, but it's hard to see anything and it smells like something died in the storm drain, which come to think of it, it probably did. Rats or worse.

"Down there," Freak says. "The beam is hitting it right now."

"That? That's just a piece of junk."

"Wrong," Freak says, real fierce. "It *looks* like a piece of junk. It may very well contain fabulous wealth. Drop the line down and see if you can hook it."

I'm thinking, boy, what a butthead, rolling in the

dirt for this little Darth Vader so he can play pretend games in the middle of the night, but I do what he asks, I drop the hook down, and much to my surprise, it actually hooks into something and when I pull up on the kite string I can see what it is.

"A purse," I say. "Looks like a grotty old purse."

"Careful," freak says. "Pull it up to the grate so I can grab the strap."

I bring it up an inch at a time, and Darth – excuse me, Freak – manages to get his small hand down through the grate and grab hold of the soggy old purse and then he almost drops it. I yank it up on the kite string and we both manage to squeeze the slimy purse up through the bars.

"Whew! Mission accomplished," Freak says.

The old purse is torn and wet, and I don't want to touch it unless I have gloves on.

"Gross," I say. "Somebody must have flushed this down a toilet."

"No way," Freak says. "I saw one of Tony D.'s punks stuff it down there yesterday morning."

"Yeah? They must have stole it."

"No doubt," Freak says, and he opens the clasp and points his little light inside the purse.

By now I know there isn't going to be any treasure, but still this is pretty cool, recovering stuff that Blade's gang ripped off from some little old lady or whatever.

"A wallet," Freak says, and he flips open this cheap-looking wallet, the kind that's made to hold credit cards.

There's no money inside, but there is a plastic ID card, and on the plastic card is a lady's name.

"Loretta Lee," Freak says. "I'll bet you anything she's a damsel in distress."

Which, as it turns out, is almost true. The real deal is that she's a damsel who *causes* distress. Which we find out the very next day.

# The Damsel of Distress 11

The address on the ID card is this place on the other side of the millpond. They used to call it the New Tenements, but now everybody mostly calls it the New Testaments, which Gram told me has nothing to do with the Bible.

"People will make their jokes," she says. "Call that place whatever you want, but you are not to set foot there. Is that clear, Maxwell dear?"

It's not like I *wanted* to go into the Testaments, so it was real easy to keep that promise, and then the day after we pull that soggy purse out of the sewer Freak explains how it's okay to break a promise if you're on a quest.

"There may even be a reward involved," he says.

"The lady won't have much money if she lives in the Testaments," I say. "Poor people live there, and dope fiends."

What we do is go down to the playground and cut over behind that little patch of trees, just in case anybody is looking, and then we can circle around behind the pond. Freak is riding up top, which he almost always does now. That way he doesn't have to wear his leg brace or carry his crutches, and besides, I like how it feels to have a really smart brain on my shoulders, helping me think.

Freak is talking a mile a minute, more stuff about the Round Table and how important quests are, and why knights are bound up with oaths, which is not the same thing as swearing, and I'm trying to listen and not ask questions because if I ask questions, he'll pull out his dictionary.

When we get to the Testaments, though, Freak shuts right up. It's this big, falling-apart place with a bunch of apartments, and it looks sad and smells like fish and sour milk. There're a lot of bikes and toys lying around, mostly bashed up and broken, and the little kids who live there look almost as busted up as the toys. When they see us coming they make these screaming noises and run away, but you can tell they're not really scared, they just want to pretend like we're a monster or something, eek eek.

"Maybe we should reconsider this particular

quest," Freak says. He's up there on my shoulders and he's getting fidgety, squirming around.

But we're already outside the apartment door, and I go, "Maybe she really needs that ID card," so it's my fault what happens next.

The door opens before we even ring the bell, and this hand comes snaking out and reaches for the mailbox and finds this rolled-up newspaper and pulls it back inside. And there's something about the blind way that hand moves that's creepy. Get me out of here, I'm thinking.

Then, before I can get my feet moving fast enough to leave, this woman's voice is cussing us out.

"Iggy!" she says. "Iggy, come here and see this!"

Now she's standing in the doorway, this scrawny, yellow-haired woman with small, hard eyes and blurry red lips. She's wearing this ratty old bathrobe and she's smoking this cigarette and squinting at us and making a face.

"Iggy," she says out of the side of her mouth, "come here and tell me is the circus in town or what?"

Next thing there's this big hairy dude in the doorway, he's got a huge beer gut and these giant arms all covered with blue tattoos and he's got a beard that looks like it's made out of red barbed wire.

"Ain't the circus," he says, spitting a big gob on the step. "This here is the carnival."

Freak isn't saying anything, and I want to get out of here, so I go, "Sorry, wrong number," and I'm trying to back away and not fall over a tricycle when the hairy dude comes out the door real quick and gets in my way.

"Not so fast," he says. "Who sent you?"

"I know the big one," the woman is saying. She's waving her cigarette around and squinting her eyes up and you can tell she's thinking of something, worrying it like a dog with a bone. "I seen him around somewhere. Don't he look familiar, Iggy? Don't he?"

Freak finally says, "Please excuse us, we have the wrong address. We were, uhm, trying to locate a Miss Loretta Lee."

The tattoo dude hears that and he starts to laugh, this fat sound way down in his big belly, and he goes, "You hear that, Loretta? This an old flame of yours or what?" Then he reaches up and pokes me in the chest hard enough to make me catch my breath, and he says, "Cat got your tongue, kid? What is this, a Siamese-twin act?"

All I can think to say is, "Oops," because we have

the right address after all. The squinty woman in the robe is Loretta Lee, and even more important, Iggy is Iggy Lee, and I feel like a total butthead because I've heard of Iggy Lee, he's the boss of The Panheads, this bad-news motorcycle gang.

"We found your purse!" Freak blurts out, and he tosses down the purse and Iggy Lee catches it with one hand and he gives Loretta this secret look, like he's going to have some fun here.

"You better come inside," he says, looking up at Freak. "You and Frankenstein."

"Sorry," Freak says, and his voice is chattery high. "We'll have to decline your kind invitation because we, uhm, we have to leave now."

Loretta flicks her cigarette butt at my feet and she says, "Iggy says come inside, you better do it."

So we go inside. I have to take Freak off my shoulders so we can get in the door and that's when Loretta looks at me real hard and she says, "I know that one. It's like a flash from the past, Iggy. You know him?"

Iggy isn't paying any attention to her, he's pointing at this ratty chair and he says, "Sit down, it makes me nervous looking up."

Loretta comes around and she says, "Don't be making Iggy nervous. Not this early in the day. Last dude made him nervous, they had to—"

"Shut up, Loretta," Iggy says in this real quiet voice. "I'm thinking. You're right, he *does* look familiar."

I'm sitting in this chair, which feels like it might bust apart, and Freak is right next to me and I can see he's trying to stand straight but it's not easy because he's all bent up inside.

"Names," Iggy says.

Freak clears his throat and tries to make his voice sound deep and more grown up. "We're sorry to disturb you, but we have to go home now. It's a matter of some urgency."

Iggy reaches out and he flicks his fingers at Freak's nose, *whack*. I can tell it hurts, but Freak doesn't say anything, he just tenses up.

Iggy goes, "I ask a question, you better answer, get it? Names. I want your names."

Freak tells his name and then mine and Iggy reaches down and pats him on the head. "Very good," he says. "Now that wasn't hard, was it? Next question, where'd you get Loretta's purse?"

Freak tells him we found it in the storm drain. He doesn't mention us dressing up all in black, or the Darth Vader costume, or anything about knights or quests.

"Next question," Iggy says. "Where's the money?"

Loretta coughs on her new cigarette and says, "But Iggy, there wasn't any money," and he goes, "Shut up, Loretta," and she coughs again and shuts up, you can tell she's afraid of Iggy, the way she holds herself tight whenever he says anything.

Freak goes, "I've got two dollars in change, you can have it but we have to go home now."

Iggy gives him this look like he's thinking seriously about throwing up and he says, "What is it with you, you've gotta go home? We're having a nice little talk here, don't spoil it."

All of a sudden Loretta jumps up and she goes, "Iggy! Iggy! I've got it! Kenny Kane! Remember Kenny Kane?"

For a second I think he's going to hit her, and then he relaxes and really looks at me and his eyes go wide and he nods and says, "Sure. That's it. Kenny Kane. You're right, he's a ringer for old Killer Kane. Must be his kid, huh? Sure it is."

Loretta looks real happy that she finally figured it out and she runs into the kitchen and kicks some stuff out of the way and pulls open the refrigerator and we can hear her laughing and saying, "I *knew* it, I just *knew* it."

When she comes back in she's got two cans of

Bud and she pops them both and gives one to Iggy. "Breakfast of champions," she says. "What a flash, huh? You remember that time old Kenny—"

"Shut up, Loretta!" Iggy says, then he chugs the Bud and squashes the can in his fist and he drops it right on the floor. Which is the first time I notice all the other crushed cans, they're everywhere, the whole place is like a trash can or a big ashtray or something.

Meanwhile Freak is giving me this look like he has no idea what's going on, and that look scares me more than Iggy Lee and all his tattoos.

"I've got him, too," Loretta says, snapping her fingers. "The midget or dwarf or whatever he is. He must be Gwen's kid, you remember Gwen? Stuck-up Gwen?"

"No," Iggy says, and his eyes are burning into me. "Never heard of Gwen."

Loretta goes, "Doesn't matter. What a flash this is. Kenny Kane. Time flies, huh, Ig? I can remember when these two were *born*. And then, what was it, a couple of years later Kenny does his thing and he's in the yard, right? Doing time."

Iggy says, "That he is. I know a guy knows him inside." He gives me this creepy look and he says, "You go up there to visit the old man, you tell him Iggy says hello, okay?"

"I doubt he even *knows* his father, Ig. He was only a little kid when it happened. Right?"

I don't say anything and Freak is looking at me like he's never seen me before and then Iggy says, "Killer Kane. What a tough hombre *he* was."

Loretta says, "I heard he seen the light in there. He's got religion, is that true?"

"I don't know."

Iggy snorts and says, "He don't know. You don't know much, do you?"

I shake my head.

Loretta says, "He's some kinda retard, Ig. He don't even know how big and strong he is, I'll bet." She pokes Iggy or tickles him and in this strange giggly voice she says, "Whyn't you find out? Find out if he's as strong as he looks?"

Iggy scowls and goes, "Give me a break, Loretta." He gives me this long look and then he hooks his thumb at the door and says, "Show time is over, boys. Get out of here, the both of you."

Loretta says, "But, Iggy, we could have some fun."

"You're the retard, Loretta," Iggy says. "What if Killer Kane hears I was messing with his kid? No thank you."

"He's in for life," she says. "What's the harm?"

"Life ain't life, how many times I tell you that?"

Loretta is squinting at him and she goes, "Are you serious? He's getting out someday?" and Iggy looks at me and tells her to shut up again.

Finally we get to the door and that's when Loretta wants to rub Freak on the head. Real hard, with her knuckles.

"This is for luck," she says to Iggy. "It's good luck, rubbing a dwarf on the head."

Freak is trying to duck away and he says, "I'm not a dwarf and I'm not good luck."

So Loretta gives up on rubbing his head and she stands up straight and folds her arms and says, "Hey, midget man? I know all about you. Your old man was a magician, did you know that?"

Freak is scuttling around behind me, keeping out of her way, but when she says that, I can tell he wants to know about his father, if maybe he really *was* a magician.

"Yeah," Loretta says. "Right after you was born. He *must* be a magician, because as soon as he heard the magic words 'birth defect', he disappeared."

A second later Iggy shoves us out the door.

# Killer Kane, Killer Kane, 12
## Had a Kid Who Got No Brain

I feel real bad for Freak, because he hates it when people try to rub his head for luck, but I don't say a word, I just run us home, thumping the short way back around the pond, and my big feet never even trip me up because I'm on automatic, I'm this running machine.

"Whoa!" Freak says when we get to his house. "Now *that* was an adventure, huh?"

"An evil dude like Iggy Lee, we were lucky to get out of there alive."

Freak goes, "No way, that was all talk."

Yeah, right. The real deal is that I was scared the whole time I was there, and so was Freak, even if he won't admit it now.

"That stuff about my father was true," Freak says, studying his fingernails and acting real cool again.

"The Fair Gwen won't talk about it. All she says is 'He made his decision and I made mine.' But I know he ran away because of me. And you know what?"

"What?"

"Good riddance to bad rubbish."

For some reason that really gets me laughing. Something about the way he says it, or maybe it's all that nervous stuff left over from the New Testaments. Whatever, I'm rolling on the ground like a moron and Freak is strutting around and saying stuff like, "Loretta my Queen, wouldst thou accept my hand in marriage?" and "Sir Iggy, wouldst thou do us all a big favour and fall upon thy sword?" And I'm laughing so hard I can hardly breathe.

Everything is pretty much okay after that. One thing we don't do, though, we don't talk about my father, good old Killer Kane. Which is fine by me.

* * *

School.

For the last week or so it's like getting jabbed with a little needle every time I hear that word. Gram is trying to pretend how excited she is I'm finally in the eighth grade, like this is a really big deal. Which is a joke, because the only reason I got passed from seventh grade is because they figured this way the big butthead can be – quote – someone *else's* problem, thank God, we've had quite enough of Maxwell Kane – unquote.

Gram takes me out to the mall to get new clothes, which is about as much fun as going to the dentist, except maybe worse because at least at the dentist you're mostly just in a chair with the door closed, where at the mall with Gram it's like hello, world, here I am, take a good look.

This girl at the shoe store, she's got a little smirk and she goes, "Thirteen triple E? Do they make shoes that big?" and Gram goes, "I'm quite sure they do, dear, you go ask the manager." And then she looks at me and she goes, "Maxwell, this is *not* major surgery, so will you please, as a special favour to me, wipe that wounded look off your face and try to be polite."

Yeah, right. The manager, when he comes out with these Brand-X running shoes, he wants to help me take off my old shoes, like he's pretty sure I can't do it by myself, but I give him this look and he backs off and lets me do it myself.

"I wish you'd tie those laces, dear," Gram says when I'm squishing around in the new shoes.

"That's the fashion," the manager says with this heh-heh-heh laugh. "Actually, they're designed that way. You don't *need* to lace up."

Just to prove what a jerk he is, I tie up the laces and that makes Gram happy. Which is funny sometimes, how little it takes to make her happy, except you can't really figure what until you've already done it. Does that make any sense?

Finally we escape from the mall and I've got enough new clothes to last me, as Grim points out, a week or so.

"You could just keep letting down his cuffs," Grim says. "Except they don't have cuffs now, what am I thinking?"

"I think he looks quite handsome," Gram says. "Maxwell, please turn around. And keep your shirt-tail tucked in."

"Ah, leave him alone," Grim says. "He's not a fashion model."

"I just can't get over it," Gram says. "Our little Maxwell is growing up."

"Growing is right," Grim says. "The boy is certainly growing."

The deal is, Freak and I get to be in the same classes. He made the Fair Gwen go in and see all these people at the school, because I wasn't supposed to be in the smart classes, no way, and finally they all agreed it would be good for Freak, having someone to help him get around.

Gram acts kind of worried about it and she doesn't want to sign the papers, like she thinks the L.D. class has done me a lot of good or something, and being in the genius class is just going to make me slower and dumber than ever. But one night I come up the cellar stairs real quiet and Grim is saying, "Let's give it a try, nothing else has worked, maybe what he needs is a friend, that's the one thing he's never had with all those special teachers." And the next morning she signs the papers, and when we get to school the first day, Freak helps me find my name on the list and it's true, we're in all the same classes.

At first all the other kids are so into looking cool and acting cool and showing off their new outfits, they hardly notice us in the hall, Freak riding high on my shoulders, or the deal where his desk is always right next to mine. That wears off, though, and by the time we leave maths, which is just passing out the textbooks and a bunch of numbers chalked on the blackboard, you can hear the whispers in the hall.

Like, hey, who's the midget? And, there goes Mad Max; and, excuse me while I barf; and, look what escaped from the freak show; and, oh, my *gawd*, that's *disgusting*.

"Maxwell Kane?"

This is from Mrs. Donelli, the English teacher, she's new to the school, and when I nod and raise my pencil, she goes, "Maxwell, will you please stand up and tell the class something about your summer?"

Which, if she wasn't new to the school, she'd know better, because getting up in the class and saying stuff is not something I do.

"Maxwell," she goes, "is there a problem?"

By now there's a lot of noise and kids are shouting stuff like, "Forget it, Mrs. Donelli, his brain is in his tail!"

"Ask him to count, he can paw the ground!"

"Maxi Pad! Maxi Pad! Ask him quick about his dad!"

"Killer Kane! Killer Kane! Had a kid who got no brain!"

Mrs. Donelli has this look like she stepped in something and can't get it off her shoe. The shouting and singing goes on and on, and pretty soon some of the kids are throwing stuff at us, pencils and erasers and wadded-up paper, and it's like Mrs. Donelli has no idea what to do about it, the room is out of control.

Then Freak climbs up on his desk, which makes him about as big as a normal person standing up, and he starts shouting at the top of his lungs.

"Order!" he shouts. "Order in court! Let justice be heard!"

For some reason, maybe because he looks so fierce with his jaw sticking out and his little fists all balled up and the way he's stamping his crooked little feet, everybody shuts up and there's this spooky silence.

Finally Mrs. Donelli says, "You must be Kevin, is that right?"

Freak has this look, he's still acting really fierce, and he goes, "Sometimes, I am."

"Sometimes? What does that mean?"

"It means sometimes I'm *more* than Kevin."

"Oh," says Mrs. Donelli, and you can tell she has no idea what he's talking about, but she thinks it's important to let him talk. "So, Kevin," she says, "can you give us all an example?"

Next thing I know, Freak has his hands on my head and he's getting himself on my shoulders and he's tugging at me in a way that I know means "stand up", and so I do it, I stand right up in class and I can see Mrs. Donelli's eyes getting bigger and bigger.

I'm standing right there with Freak high above me

and it feels right, it makes me feel strong and smart.

"How's *this* for an example?" Freak is saying. "Sometimes we're nine feet tall, and strong enough to walk through walls. Sometimes we fight gangs. Sometimes we find treasure. Sometimes we slay dragons and drink from the Holy Grail!"

Mrs. Donelli is backing up to her desk and she says, "Oh, my, that's very interesting, I'm sure, but could you both just sit down?"

But Freak is riding me like he's the jockey and I'm the horse, he's steering me around the classroom, showing off. He's raising his fist and punching it in the air and going, "Freak the Mighty! Freak the Mighty!" and pretty soon he's got all the other kids chanting, "Freak the Mighty! Freak the Mighty! Freak the Mighty!" even though they don't know what he's talking about, or what it means.

I'm standing up straight, as tall as I can, and I'm marching exactly like he wants me to, right and left, backwards and forwards, and it's like music or something, like I don't even have to think about it, I just do it, and all those kids chanting our name, and Mrs. Donelli has no idea what's going on, she's definitely flipped out and more or less hiding behind her desk.

The whole class is raising their fists in the air and

chanting: "Freak the Mighty! Freak the Mighty! Freak the Mighty!"

I can't explain why, but it was really pretty cool.

* * *

Anyhow, that's how Freak and I get sent to the principal's office the first time together.

Mrs. Addison, she's the principal, she takes one look at us waiting outside her office, and she goes, "What have we here?"

"I'm afraid there has been a slight misunderstanding," Freak says. "If you'd be so good as to allow me to explain."

Mrs. Addison is this slightly serious-acting black woman with tight grey hair in a bun and these suits that make her look like she works in a bank or something. She has this funny little smile like she's sucking on a lemon and it quickly turns sweet, and then she goes, "By all means. Let's hear what you have to say. Convince me."

I can't really remember what Freak said, except that he used so many big words, she had to keep looking stuff up in his dictionary, which she seemed to get a real kick out of, but the important thing is, whatever Freak told her, she fell for it.

# 13 American Chop Suey

I used to think all that spooky stuff about Friday the Thirteenth was just a pile of baloney. But now I'm getting my own personal introduction to what can happen. It's October, and so far things have been going pretty good, better than I ever expected. Me and Freak are like this unit, and even Mrs. Donelli says she is starting to get used to us, which is her way of admitting that Freak is about twice as smart as she is, and for sure he's read more books.

She keeps saying stuff like, "Kevin, we *know* you know the answer, because you *always* know the answer, so wouldn't it be nice if someone else got a chance? For instance, your friend Maxwell?"

Freak goes, "He knows the answer, Mrs. Donelli."

"Yes, Kevin, and I'm sure you're correct because you're *always* correct, but for a change I'd really like to hear Maxwell speak for himself. Maxwell? Maxwell Kane?"

This is dumb because what does it matter if I know the answer? If I don't know, then Freak will tell me and he'll say it in a way I can understand, which is a lot better then Mrs. Donelli can do. So what I do, I just shrug and smile and wait, because I know she'll get tired of asking and move on to the next. As a matter of fact I *do* know the answer – the reason Johnny Tremain got mad and hateful is because he burned his hand in a stupid accident – and I know about that because Freak has been showing me how to read a whole book and for some reason it all makes sense, where before it was just a bunch of words I didn't care about.

My reading skills tutor, Mr. Meehan, he says stuff like, "Max, the tests have always shown that you're not dyslexic or disabled, and this proves it. As you know, heh heh, my personal opinion has always been that you're lazy and stubborn and you didn't *want* to learn. So if hanging out with Kevin somehow improves your attitude and your skills, that's great. Keep up the good work."

It was Mr. Meehan who had a word with Mrs. Donelli, and that's why she finally gave up on trying to make me talk in class, and instead she waits until study hall, where she asks me the same questions alone and I tell her the answers. She still doesn't get it, though, because she always goes, "But, Maxwell, if you can speak to me, then you can speak to your classmates, right?"

Wrong. Big difference. I can't explain what it is, except that my mouth shuts up when there's more than one or two people, and a whole classroom full, forget it.

"Okay, you're shy about public speaking, but how does that apply to writing down the answers? If you can read, then you can write, right?"

Wrong again. The reading stuff Freak helped me figure out by showing how words are just voices on paper. Writing down the words is a whole different story. No matter what Freak says, writing the stuff down is not like talking, and my hand feels so huge and clumsy, it's like the pencil is a piece of spaghetti or something and it keeps slipping away.

Mrs. Donelli says okay for now, she's satisfied I can read, but we'll really have to work on this writing thing, won't we, Maxwell, and when she says that, I just nod and look away, because inside I'm thinking, forget it, no way.

Like Freak says, reading is just a way of listening, and I could always listen, but writing is like talking, and that's a whole other ball game.

Anyhow, what happens first on Friday the Thirteenth, we're in homeroom when this note comes from the principal's office:

*Maxwell Kane, your presence is requested.*

Gulp.

So Freak and I get up to go and the teacher says, "No, Kevin, you stay here. Mrs. Addison was very specific. Maxwell is to go alone."

Freak starts to smart-mouth her, then he changes his mind and he nudges me and whispers, "Just give 'em your name, rank, and serial number. Deny everything. You aren't back by ten hundred hours, we'll organize a search-and-rescue mission."

He offers to lend me his dictionary, in case I want to try out any big words on Mrs. Addison, but I'm already so worried about being called in alone, all I can think is they're going to put me back in the learning disabled class. I've already decided I'll run away if they do that, I'll go live in the woods somewhere and jump out and scare people. Anyhow, I don't take Freak's dictionary along because my hands are trembly and I might drop it, or Mrs. Addison might ask me a word and I'll forget how to look it up and prove I'm still a butthead goon.

Mrs. Addison is waiting outside her office, like she does, and she's trying to smile but she's not really a smiling kind of person and I can tell this is serious, whatever it is.

Like maybe somebody died.

I go, "Gram! Is Gram okay?"

"Yes, yes, everybody is fine. Come in and sit down, Maxwell. And please try to relax."

Yeah, right.

Mrs. Addision is sitting there in her big chair and she's looking up at the ceiling and then she's looking at the floor, and at her hands, and finally she gets around to looking at me. "This is rather difficult, Maxwell. I don't know where to begin. First, let me say we're all pleased with your progress. It's nothing short of miraculous, and it almost convinces me you knew how to read at your level all along and were for some reason keeping it a secret."

I'm not really hearing what she's saying because there's like this little bird fluttering around inside my chest, and it makes me blurt out: "You're putting me back in L.D., right?"

Mrs. Addison comes over and pats me on the shoulder. I can tell it makes her nervous, touching me, but she does it anyway, and she goes, "No, no.

Nothing like that. This has nothing to do with school, Maxwell. This is a personal situation."

"Because if I have to go back in the L.D. class, I won't. I just won't. I'll run away. I will, I will."

"Maxwell, this is *not* about your class work, or even about school. This is about your, uhm, father."

My, uhm, father. Which makes me wish all of a sudden I'd done something wrong and Mrs. Addison was just giving me detention.

She takes a deep breath and folds her hands together like she's praying and she says, "A request has been forwarded to me from the parole board. A request from your father. Maxwell, your father wants to know if—"

"I don't want to hear it!"

I jump up and cover my ears, holding my hands real tight. "Don't want to hear it! Don't want to hear it! Don't! Don't! Don't!"

What happens when you go nuts in the principal's office, she calls in the school nurse, and the two of them are trying to hug me and calm me down, and it's like I'm back in day care or something.

"Maxwell?" Mrs. Addison is saying. She's trying to prise my hands away from my ears. "Maxwell, please forget about it, okay? Forget I said it. You don't have to do anything you don't want to do, okay? And I'll make sure of that, I promise. I swear on my honour, he can't make you do anything you don't want to do. I'm going to make that *very* clear to the parole board, and to his lawyer. Very clear indeed."

Finally I take my hands off my ears, which wasn't really working because I could still hear everything they said, and big surprise, I'm sitting in the corner of the room, down on the floor with my knees all hunched up, and I don't even remember how I got here.

It's like I blanked out or something, and the nurse is giving me this cup of water, and the weird thing is she's crying.

"I'm sorry," I say. "I didn't mean to hurt you."

"You didn't," she says. "I cry easily, don't you worry about it."

I do worry about it though, because if she's crying, I must have hit her and I don't remember it. Which, if you think about it, is *really* scary.

Who knows what I might do and then not remember it?

\* \* \*

The worst thing happens later, in the cafeteria.

Freak has this thing about American chop suey. He *loves* the stuff. The gooier the better. You'd never believe a person so small could eat so much, and when he holds up his plate, he always says, "Please, sir, more gruel," and I always say, "It's American chop suey, not gruel, I looked up gruel, remember?" and he always goes, "I beg of you, sir, more gruel!" and so finally I go up to get him another helping.

When I come back, something is wrong. Freak's face is all red and swollen up and he's making this huk-huk-huk noise. He can't talk, all he can do is look at me and try to say something with his eyes and then I'm running to get the nurse.

"Quick. He can't breathe! He can't breathe!"

Then she's running as fast as me and she's yelling for someone to call an ambulance.

Back in the cafeteria, Freak is turning purple. The nurse grabs him and she's got this plastic thing she shoves into his mouth and his eyes are closed up tight and one of his legs is kicking.

I don't know what to do so I start hopping up and down in one place, and when the kids keep crowding around I push them back, and the next thing Freak's face is starting to look pink instead of purple and he's breathing okay.

Right about then the ambulance comes, I never even heard the siren, and Freak is trying to talk in this croaky voice as they put him on the stretcher. "I'm okay," he keeps saying. "Really, I'm okay, I just want to go home."

The deal is, once they call the ambulance, you have to go to the hospital and get checked out, that's a rule. I keep trying to get into the back of the ambulance with him, but they won't let me. Finally Mrs. Addison has to come out and pull me away until the ambulance leaves with just the light going and not the siren.

"You've had quite a day, haven't you?" she says, walking me back into the school.

"It's not me who had quite a day," I say. "Kevin is the one. All he did was try and eat his lunch."

Mrs. Addison gives me this look, and then she goes, "You're going to be okay, Maxwell Kane. I'm sure of it now."

She's okay for a principal, but for some reason I still can't make her understand that it's not me who had a really bad Friday the Thirteenth.

And I swear on the dictionary, if Freak ever tries to eat American chop suey again, I'll dump it on his head or something.

# Cross My Heart 14
and Hope to Die

Gram lets me stay home the next day because Freak is getting out of the hospital, and I'm right on the front step when the Fair Gwen pulls up in her car. Freak is riding in the back, you can barely see him in the window, and he's got this big grin that makes me feel like everything is going to be okay, the way everybody keeps saying.

I go, "Is it okay if I carry him inside?" and the Fair Gwen says, "Of course."

"He has to rest," she says. "He stays in the house until I say different, is that understood?"

In his room, Freak is right away ordering me around, bring me this and go do that, and you'd never guess he's been sick.

"A minor incident," he says. "Easily corrected by biogenic intervention."

"You mean that robot stuff?"

Freak goes, "Sssssh! The Fair Gwen must not know of the plan. The very idea strikes fear into her heart."

"Well it is pretty scary," I say, "getting an operation to give you a whole new body."

"I'm not scared," Freak says. "I'm looking forward to it."

"So when does it happen?"

Freak gets this faraway look and he says, "I'm not sure. Dr. Spivak, she's my doctor, she says maybe a year or two."

"But how come you need a new body?" I ask. "How come you can't just stay like you are?"

Freak shakes his head, like he knows I'm not smart enough to understand. "No one stays like they are," he says. "Everybody is always changing. My problem is, I'm growing on the inside but not the outside."

He doesn't want to talk about it any more, which is fine with me. And in another couple of days, everything is back to normal and we're going to school like always, and everything is going real good until Christmas vacation when, if you'll excuse the expression, all hell breaks loose.

* * *

I'm in the down under, trying to get the stupid wrapping paper to cover the stupid presents I got for Gram and Grim, when this shouting starts upstairs.

Understand, Grim *never* yells at Gram, not that I can ever remember, and Gram, well, the worst thing she ever does is cry when she's mad. But *somebody* sure is yelling up there, and so I sneak up the stairs and I don't even have to put my ear to the door, that's how loud it is.

*"Over my dead body you will!"*

That's Gram yelling, and her voice is big and full of tears. Grim's voice isn't nearly as loud, and I open the door a crack to hear whatever it is that's made Gram so mad at him.

"I have an obligation," he's saying. "A man has to protect his family."

"Not with a gun!" Gram yells. "Not in this house! I won't have it! Oh, I can't stand it. How could they do this to us? How *could* they?"

"He fooled 'em," Grim is saying. "Just like he fooled Annie. Just like he fooled us once upon a time. Never again, though. That man tries to set foot in this house, I aim to shoot him."

"No guns," Gram says. "You don't know about guns."

"Of course I do. I was in the army, wasn't I?"

**99**

"That was thirty years ago! I know what will happen, don't you think I've dreamed about it for the last eight years? He'll come in here and he'll take that gun away from you, and then *he'll* do the shooting."

By now I've figured out who they're talking about, and I guess you have, too. None other than *Him*. Killer Kane, my father.

"Maybe they won't let him out," Gram is saying. "If they do, they'll give us protection."

"Sure they will," Grim says. "Just like they protected our Annie."

Next thing, Gram is crying, and you can tell Grim is trying to make her feel better, going, "There, there, my dear. I know, I know. There, there."

A while later, I hear the cellar stairs creaking. It's Grim, and he knocks on my door.

"Come on in."

Grim comes inside and for once he doesn't tell me what a rat hole I'm living in, or how it smells like a locker room because I forgot to put my socks in the hamper. He sits on the edge of the bed and folds his hands together. I never think about how old he is because he never acts old, but tonight he's all white and bent and his skin is saggy. He's about a thousand years old, and he says, "I guess you heard the ruckus? Your gramma gets so upset, bless her heart. Can't abide the idea of violence. Can't say I blame her."

"Did he escape?" I ask. "Is that what happened?"

Grim shakes his head. "He's up for parole."

"That's dumb. That's so dumb."

Grim goes, "You hit the nail on the head, son. What I did do, just so you know, I went into court and made it so he won't be allowed within a mile of this house. If he *does* try to come here, they'll send him back to prison, the judge promised me that much."

I say, "Maybe you *should* get a gun."

Grim doesn't say anything for quite a while, and then he goes, "Maybe I will, maybe I won't. I can't tell your gramma about it, though, and it breaks my heart to lie to her. That's one thing we've never done."

"I won't tell."

Grim is quiet again, and then he stands up from my bed and in this real old, tired voice he says, "Everything is going to be okay, Max. I'll make sure of it. But for the next few days I want you to stay in the house. Promise me you'll do that?"

"Cross my heart," I say. "Cross my heart and hope to die."

# 15 What Came Down the Chimney

Christmas Eve is real quiet. Like Freak says, "You could hear a mouse fart." Which, even if it is a stupid joke, makes Grim smile and shake his head.

Freak and the Fair Gwen have supper with us, and we're all trying to pretend like everything is normal, and nobody says a word about Killer Kane getting out of prison. The Fair Gwen is wearing this dark red silky blouse and a long black skirt that almost touches the floor, and her waist is so small, she looks like one of those Christmas ornaments, the kind that makes a tingle-bell sound when the branches move.

Freak is all dressed up, too, he's wearing this tweedy new suit jacket that has patches on the elbows and Grim says all he needs is a pipe and he'll look like quite the professor.

"No tobacco," Freak says. "Nicotine is a toxic waste of time."

"Just the pipe," Grim insists. "You don't have to smoke it."

"Don't get him started on bad habits," Gram says. "Maxwell, pass the mint sauce."

Mint sauce is one of Gram's specialities, and you'd be amazed how it improves everything, which is why I've been keeping it close by. Anyhow, the food is the best, you can't beat Gram for Christmas or Thanksgiving or birthdays, and we all eat until we're fit to bust, except the Fair Gwen makes sure Freak doesn't eat too fast.

"You'd think I was starving him," the Fair Gwen says.

"Please, sir, more gruel," he says, holding up his plate and making a funny face where his tongue sticks out sideways, and Gram laughs so hard, she has a coughing fit, which makes us all shut up.

After supper we sit around like you do, admiring the tree and talking about how lucky we are not to be homeless, and Grim starts telling these old stories about when he was a kid and they got lumps of coal in their stockings.

"If we were lucky, we got an apple core," he says, "or a few orange rinds."

"Now, Arthur," Gram says. "You never got a lump of coal in your life."

"You're right. We never even *got* a lump of coal, can you imagine? My father couldn't afford coal, so he'd write the word 'coal' on a piece of paper and put it in our stockings and we'd *pretend* it was a lump of coal, that's how poor we were."

The Fair Gwen is laughing to herself and shaking her head.

Gram says, "How can you tell such lies on Christmas Eve?"

"I'm telling tales, my dear, not lies. Lies are mean things, and tales are meant to entertain."

And so we all sit there acting polite and listening to Grim make up stuff no one would ever in a million years believe, and all of us have a cup of hot chocolate and a piece of Russell Stover candy right out of the box, and then it's time to pass around a few of the presents.

Gram has this rule that you can open one on Christmas Eve and you save the rest for morning. Which can be tough, deciding what to open first. Grim always starts it off because, like he says, he's really a kid at heart and he can't stand to wait.

From Gram he gets this woolly sweater that buttons up the front and he acts surprised, even though he's got about a hundred just like it already. Then Gram opens her present from me, which is a bracelet made of shells from beaches around the world, and she right away puts it on and says it's just what she wanted. Which is so like Gram – if you gave her an old beer can she'd act pleased and say it was just what she wanted.

Then Freak opens his present from me and even before he gets the paper all the way off, he gives me this thumbs-up and says, "Cool." It's a gizmo that looks like a jackknife, but really it's a whole bunch of little screwdrivers and wrenches and even a little magnifying glass. I'm pretty sure Freak can invent stuff with it if he feels like it.

Gram gives the Fair Gwen this scarf that just happens to match her blouse, and everybody goes ooh and ahh, and then I finally decide what present to open. Right away you'd know it was something Freak did, because the box isn't square, it's pointed at the top like a pyramid, and instead of regular wrapping paper, he's got Sunday comics taped all over it, and it's driving me nuts trying to figure out what would fit inside a pyramid-shaped box.

Freak seems like he's just as excited as me, even though he already knows what he put inside. "Take off all the paper first," he says. "There's a special way to open it."

Real careful, I peel off all the paper, and the thing is, it's not a pyramid-shaped box he bought somewhere, he *made* it. You can see where he cut out the pieces of cardboard and taped them all together, and written on the sides of the pyramid are these little signs and arrows.

"Follow the arrows," he says.

The arrows point all over the place and I have to keep turning the pyramid around, until finally I get to this sign that says:

### PRESS HERE AND BE AMAZED

"Go on," Freak says. "It's not an explosive device, silly – it won't blow up in your face."

I press the spot on the pyramid and all of a sudden, all four sides fold down at the same time and I'm looking inside the pyramid and, just like Freak promised, I'm amazed.

"The young man is a genius," Grim is saying. "And I don't use that word lightly."

Grim is right about that, because Freak has the whole thing rigged with these elastic bands and paper clips, which is what made the sides unfold all at the same time, and inside is this little platform and on the platform is a book. Not a normal book, like you buy in the store, but a book he made himself, you can tell that right away. It looks so special, I'm afraid to pick it up or I might ruin it.

"What I did was take all my favourite words," Freak says, "and put them in alphabetical order."

"Like a dictionary?"

"Exactly," Freak says, "but different, because this is *my* dictionary. Go on and look inside."

I open up the book the way he asks, and the pages smell like a ballpoint pen. It starts with A, just like a regular dictionary, but as Freak said, it's different.

## A

AARDVARK, a silly-looking creature that eats ants
AARGH, what the aardvark says when it eats ants
ABACUS, a finger-powered computer
ABSCISSA, the horizontal truth

"You don't have to read them all tonight," Freak says. "Save some for tomorrow. I gotta tell you, though, you're gonna flip when you see what I did with the Z's."

This is the best, getting Freak's dictionary. Everything else is extra.

* * *

I figure it will take for ever to fall asleep, because my head is full of stuff. Grim and his written-down lump of coal, the pyramid with the special book inside, and how fat, wet flakes of snow were falling when the Fair Gwen towed Freak home in his American Flyer wagon, and the way he was pretending to boss her by saying, "On Donner! On Dasher! On Guinevere!" and she's telling him to shut up or she'll leave him outside until he turns into a snowman.

Which must be why I'm dreaming about a little snowman who looks like Freak. The snowman keeps saying, "Cool. Cool." And when I wake up, I can feel the cold coming into my bedroom. Which is weird, because it's always warm in the down under, with the furnace right next door.

I think I hear the wind right there in the room.

Except it's not the wind.

Someone breathing.

Someone who rises up darker than night, as big as the room, and puts a giant hand on my face and presses down.

"Don't say a word, boy," he whispers. "Not a sound."

I try to move, try to shrink back into the bed, but the hand follows me down. The hand is so hard and strong I can't move, and it feels like my heart has stopped beating, it's waiting to see what will happen next.

"I came back," he says. "Like I promised."

# 16 A Chip off the Old Block

Once on the TV this dude hypnotized a lobster. Maybe you saw it. He touches a lobster and it freezes, it can't move. That's sort of what happens to me when his hand clamps over my mouth. Like I'm paralysed and my head is empty and all there is in the world is that big hand and this cool breath like the wind.

"So this is where the geezers stuck you, huh?" he whispers. "Down in the basement, out of sight, out of mind?"

I still can't see his face, he's this huge shape in the room.

"Everything changes now," he says. "It's time I got to know my own son, who had his mind poisoned against me."

He makes me sit up and shushes me to make sure

I won't make any noise. Making noise is the last thing I want to do, because I don't know whether or not Grim ever bought that gun he mentioned, or what might happen to him if he tries to use it. Gram's bad dream about Grim getting shot with his own gun seems pretty real right now, and I don't want to be the one to make it come true.

"I know what they told you," he says. "It's all a big lie, you understand? I never killed anybody, and that's the truth, so help me God."

By now I'm sitting up on the bed and he's making me put on my clothes and the weird thing is, none of this is a surprise. Somehow I always knew this would happen, that he would come for me, in the night, that I would wake up to find him there, filling the room, and that I'd feel empty.

I'm so weak, I can hardly put my shoes on. Like when you wake up and your arm is still asleep and you can't hardly make it move? That's what I feel like all over – numb and prickly and as light as a balloon. Like my hands might float up in the air if I let them.

"This'll be an adventure," he says. "You're going to have the time of your life, boy. Okay, we're leaving, and not a peep out of you."

The bulkhead door is open, and you can see the stars. Some people think the stars look close enough to touch, but Freak says the sky is like a photograph from a billion years ago, it's just some old movie they're showing up there and lots of those stars have switched off by now. They're already dead, and what we're seeing is the rerun. Which makes sense if you think about it. Someday the rerun will come to an end and you'll see all the stars start to flick off, like a billion little flames blown out by the wind.

"This way," he says. "Quiet as a mouse."

There's snow on the ground. Not a lot, enough to cover the ground. I can tell how cold the air is, but I can't feel it, even without a jacket, which I didn't have time to put on. The cold doesn't matter. Nothing does, really, not Grim and Gram or the old stars in the sky, or Freak and the Fair Gwen. They're all just make-believe, this dream I was having for a long time, and now I'm awake again and he's still filling the room somehow, even though we're outside.

The lights are out at Freak's house, and I'm thinking: *The stars clicked off* and I don't even know why I'm thinking that, it's like a dead voice in my head or something.

* * *

We're under a streetlight when he says, "Let me look at you."

He's got these big eyebrows that make it hard to see his eyes and that's fine, I don't want to see them, looking at those eyes is *asking* to have a bad dream.

"My, my," he says, checking me out. "Will you look at this? It's like I'm looking at an old picture of myself. You really *are* a chip off the old block, you know that?"

I don't say anything, and he reaches out and touches my face real gentle, as if he'd never hurt a fly. "I say, boy, do you know that? Answer me now."

"Yes, sir," I say. "Everybody says so."

"Christmas Eve," he says. "You know how many Christmas Eves I've been deprived of my own blood kin? Now is that fair, to do that to a man? Lock him up for a crime he never did?"

He's waiting for me to answer, and I say, "No, sir, not fair."

"That's over and done now," he says. "We're starting fresh. Just you and me, boy, that's how it was meant to be."

I'm standing under the streetlight and it's amazing how quiet it is. Like everybody went away or died. The quiet is almost as big as he is. He's as tall as me, only wider everywhere, and for some reason, maybe because we're not far from Freak's house, I'm thinking this weird thought: *He doesn't need a suit of armour.*

No, and he doesn't need a horse, or a lance, or a pledge to the king, or the love of a fair lady. He doesn't need anything except what he is. He's everything all rolled into one, and no one can ever beat him, not even the brave Lancelot.

He's squinting around, his eyebrows are furrowed shadows, and he says, "You know what I think of when I see a neighbourhood like this? Hamsters, is what I think. That's how these people live, like hamsters in cages. They have their little wheels to run on and that's what they do for the whole of their lives, they run and get nowhere. They just spin."

I stand there.

"They poisoned you against me, I know that," he says. "Give it time, you'll see the truth."

He starts walking fast and I walk with him, like my feet already know where to go. We're cutting through the side streets and heading down to the pond, all cold and white and frozen. Tomorrow morning a bunch of kids will take their new sledges and skates out there, and probably lose their mittens and scarfs and get yelled at by their moms and dads, but tonight the pond is empty as the moon, as empty as my head.

Once a car goes by real slow around the pond, and I've got this strange feeling there's no one at the wheel.

He hooks his finger in my shirt collar and makes me duck down until the car goes by.

The car passes and you can't see through the dark windows and you can hear the snow crunching under the tyres, squeaky and frozen.

"We're invisible," he says, making me stand up. "Now now, isn't that a kick in the pants?"

My feet already know where we're going. The New Testaments. There're a few lights on in the old buildings, and you can see some of the windows are cracked, it looks like a knife cut against the light, and he's saying, "You know about Mary and Joseph, how they sought shelter in Bethlehem, and how the baby Jesus was born in a manger?"

I try to nod and the funny thing is, even though I'm not cold, my teeth are chattering, so it's like the rest of me is freezing but my head hasn't noticed.

"That's what we're doing, seeking shelter," he says. "Except this isn't exactly a manger we're going to."

"No, sir," I say. "It sure isn't."

He touches me real soft on the back of the neck and says, "I didn't ask you a question, boy. Rule number one, don't sass your old man."

I make sure my mouth stays shut. We're coming up on the Testaments and they look almost pretty with the new snow coating the roofs and making the yards clean and white and soft. You can see where an old bike handlebar is coming up though the snow, and shapes of other things left out, and even the old car up on blocks looks new, like it might take off into the air without any wheels.

I know where we're going, even though he doesn't tell me.

The door opens before we get there, and Loretta Lee is standing in the light and she's saying, "Iggy! Come look what the cat dragged in."

He says, "Say hello to my boy, Loretta. Isn't he a chip off the old block?"

Then we're inside, and Iggy is there bolting the door behind us and closing the shades, and Loretta, she's wearing this real slinky red dress that looks like it might fall off if she sneezed, she's saying, "Mission accomplished, hey, Kenny? I knew you could do it, if anybody could."

Iggy says, "Watch your mouth, Loretta."

"I do believe you've been drinking," my father

says. "Has she been drinking, Iggy? I thought I made myself clear."

"Hey, it's Christmas Eve," Iggy says, and he sounds real nervous. "A little punch, what can it hurt?"

"A little punch," Loretta says, and her voice is slurpy. "That's all."

She's wearing these fake eyelashes and they're coming loose, so her eyes look almost as blurry as her red mouth. I know because she keeps flapping her eyes at me and smiling so I can see where the lipstick got on her teeth.

Iggy says, "She's okay, Kenny, you got my word."

"Oh *right*," Loretta says. "Turned over a new leaf, Preacher Kane turned over a new leaf so there's no booze for *anybody* on Christmas Eve, even in our own house where a man is his castle."

"Oh, shut it," Iggy says, and he makes Loretta sit down on the busted couch, where she kind of leans over and waves at me, wink wink.

"Bring me and my boy some food," my father says. "We've been out in the cold for eight long years and we're hungry, aren't we, son?"

"Yes, sir," I say.

Iggy goes out into the kitchen to fry up some hamburgers and we sit there waiting, not saying anything. Loretta is snuggled up on the couch, passed out with this dreamy look on her face.

I eat that greasy hamburger, even though I can hardly stand to swallow, and Iggy is fussing around like it's such a big deal, having Kenny Kane in the house, and it's hard to believe he's the same Iggy who is boss of The Panheads, this motorcycle gang that strikes fear into the hearts of everybody, including the cops.

Then Loretta wakes up and stretches like a cat, yawning so you can practically see right down her throat, and she says, "I guess I needed that." Then she giggles, hiding her mouth. "I guess I need a lot of things."

My father wipes his mouth with his folded paper napkin and he ignores her and looks at Iggy and says, "You ever do time, you could be a cook."

Iggy gives this nervous heh heh heh, like wouldn't that be fun, being a cook in prison. He says, "Any time you want, I'll show you that place I told you about."

My father stands up. "Now is good," he says. He looks right at me. "Come on, boy."

# By All That's Holy 17

There's a back alley between the tenement buildings, you can't see it from the road, and Iggy takes us along the alley to this other place. You can tell how the door has been busted in and the lock broke, and we go into the dark hallway.

The lights come on and the first thing I notice is the perfume an old lady wears, and the smell of cats.

"It ain't much, but the old bat who lives here took the Greyhound to visit her sister for the holiday," Iggy says. He's trying to smile.

The little room is warm and close-feeling, and the furniture is real old and saggy. There's a big old TV with a doily on the top, and an empty goldfish bowl, and piles of newspapers tied up neat with string, and a Bible on this little table by the TV. Also there's this trick picture of Jesus on the wall, where his eyes keep following you, and you go cross-eyed looking at it.

"Ain't much worth taking," Iggy says.

My father is looking around, making sure the curtains are closed. "You think I'd steal from an old woman?" he says.

Iggy shakes his head. "I sure don't."

"Never you mind," my father says. "This will do in a pinch, until we get started."

"I better get back to Loretta."

"You do that."

My father watches the door shut behind Iggy and he doesn't say anything. I'm just standing there in the middle of the room because I don't know what he wants me to do.

"Make yourself comfy, boy," he finally says. "I'm going to check we have a back way out."

I'm looking at the door we came in by, just looking, when all of a sudden he's there behind me, and I feel the cool air of him on the back of my neck.

"You wouldn't light out on me now, would you?"

"No, sir, I wouldn't."

"Sit down," he says. "We need to talk, man to man."

I sit down in this old-lady chair that's so soft, I almost sink through to the floor and I'm wondering what happened to the cats. Maybe she took them with her, to visit her sister. Or maybe Iggy let them out and they can't get back in.

He leans over me and puts his big hands on the arms of the chair and he says, "Now, your grandparents say you're nothing but a dysfunctional retard, but no kin of mine is a retard, and that's a fact. So first thing, you've got to start acting smart. Use your head. We've got a situation going here, boy, so the way to handle it, you just do exactly what I say, no matter what. Understood?"

"Yes, sir."

His hand shoves through my hair and I can feel how strong he is, even though he doesn't hurt me.

"That's good," he says. "That's real good."

He goes into another room and I can hear a door banging and stuff being moved around and when he comes back, he's got this rope in his hands. "A boy who doesn't know his own father might be dumb enough to run away," he says. "We can't have that, can we?"

"No, sir."

"No, sir, what?"

"No, sir, we can't have that."

What he does is tie my feet and hands and then he loops the end of the rope around his waist.

"I'm taking sack time while I can," he says. "You're as smart as I think you are, you'll get some shut-eye, too."

He turns out the light and lies down on the floor beside the chair, with just his arm for a pillow, and for a long time I can't tell whether he's asleep or pretending. Then I decide it doesn't matter, if I move, the rope will surely wake him.

It seems like we're frozen inside that room, even though the air is warm and stuffy. The soft chair keeps a hold of me, I'm not strong enough to get up, my feet and hands are getting tingly where they're tied, and pretty soon I can't even keep my eyes open.

I'm half asleep, dreaming a cat is in the other room, mewing for milk, and I'm still thinking about that cat when something tugs me.

He's sitting there in the dark, so I can't see his face, and he says, "Wake up, sleepyhead. I better tell my own son a thing or two he needs to know about his own father. First thing, like I already said, I never killed anybody. I'm big like you're big, so folks assume things they shouldn't. You understand what I'm saying?"

"Yes, sir, I do."

"Good. Now the other thing is the geezers you've been living with all these years. I bet they never gave you the presents I sent you, did they?"

"No, sir, they didn't."

He shakes his head real sorrowful. "That's a crime, not giving a boy presents from his father. I suppose you didn't get the letters I sent? No, if they didn't give over the presents, they likely tore up the letters. Another crime against humanity, that's what *that* is. They hated me from the first sight. On account of my appearance, and because I wasn't good enough for their precious daughter. As if a man should be blamed for how fearsome or cruel he looks, when in fact he's truly a loving person inside. Which I am. I can hardly see a sad movie without crying and I'm not afraid to say so."

There's just enough streetlight coming through the curtains so I can make out part of his face when he turns it. You can see where there's a wet spot on his cheek, and he brushes it away.

"I've been locked up like an animal," he says. "Every single night I cried myself to sleep and that's a fact. Killer Kane, that's just an unkind nickname they hung on me. You know how kids can be mean in school, mean as animals? It was like that, only these weren't kids, they were adults who should know better, except they're so ignorant and hateful they believe the worst."

His voice is sort of ragged, but you can't help but listen to him, you follow the words up and down like you're riding through mountains and you can't see to either side, all you can see is the road just ahead.

"A great injustice was done to me, boy," he says. "What those people did, they stole my life. They took *years* away from me, might as well have cut out my heart with a knife, that's how it was to lie awake each night and think about the injustice was done to me. They'd blame me for all the wrongs in the world, those people. By which I mean the geezers, *her* folks that always hated me, and of course the police who failed to see the truth of the situation."

He stops to rub away another stream of tears. There's no crying in his voice, you can't hear it there, but sure enough the tears are all over his face, slick and shiny in the pale, pale light.

"I woke up just now worrying that you might wonder why I never did mention her. Your mother. You might still be thinking the wrong way on that, and believe what they told you. You being such a tiny thing when it happened, how could you know the truth of it?"

He gets up then, and he goes over by the TV set,

far enough so the rope is tugging at me. Then he's back and he's got a book in his hands.

"You know what this is, boy?"

"The Bible," I say.

"You can tell that in the dark, can you? That's fine. What I'm going to do, I'm putting my right hand down on this Bible, see?"

"Yes, sir, I see."

"And I'm putting my other hand over my heart, can you see that?"

"Yes, sir, I can."

"That's good, boy. Now listen up. I, Kenneth David Kane, do swear by all that's Holy that I did not murder this boy's mother. And if that isn't the truth, may God strike me dead."

I'm waiting to see if something happens, and nothing does. The room is the same. It smells of old-lady perfume and missing cats, and my hands and feet are still tied by a rope to his waist.

"Satisfied?" he says.

I want to answer him but my throat closes up and my tongue is so dry, I can't hardly open my mouth. I keep thinking about how heavy his hand was on that Bible.

"I asked you a question, boy."

"Yes, sir," I say. "I'm satisfied."

He lies back down after that and pretty soon he's breathing heavy again. I can't sleep, though. I just sit there like a lump until the sun comes up, trying not to think about things I didn't want to remember.

## Never Trust a Cripple 18

I'm waiting for something to happen. The whole world except me is asleep and the only sound is him breathing heavy. I'm trying to see through the curtains, out the old lady's window when it finally gets light, but the snow is stuck to the glass and everything is fuzzy, which is pretty much how I feel.

Looking down at him on the floor, how he overflows on the rug, I think about that story where a giant falls asleep and is tied up by little people. Not that I do anything. I'm just a blob in the chair with numb hands and numb feet.

Finally what happens, there's a noise from the back and these light skittery footsteps, and then my father comes awake so fast he almost yanks me from the chair.

He's on his feet with this wild look in his eye, and

Loretta Lee glides into the room.

"Merry Christmas, boys," she says. She's got this pizza box in her hands, holding it out like a present.

"Where's Iggy?" my father asks.

"Waiting for Santa Claus," Loretta says. "Ain't nothing open this morning, but we got this left over, you're welcome to it."

"Best put that down," he says, and he pulls on the rope and lifts me up. He gives her this cold look. "You go on and get Iggy," he says.

Loretta Lee is wearing this long winter coat, it looks clean and brand-new, so she probably got it for Christmas, but her legs are skinny and bare where her feet go into these old rubber boots. She's smoking this cigarette and squinting through the smoke at my father, like she's trying to figure out what he's thinking.

"Why can't you be nice, Kenny?" she says. "We had some good times in the old days, remember?"

"The old days are over," he says. "That the best you can do for us, leftover pizza?"

"Hey, pizza is good for you," she says. "It has vitamins and stuff."

"I still want to see Iggy."

Loretta takes a drag on her cigarette and she's got this crooked smile. Her eyes keep flicking at me and the way I'm roped up, but mostly she's looking at him. "Ig'll be up soon," she says. "He had himself a tough night."

"I have business with him, Loretta," he says. "Important business."

"I'm sure," she says, and she turns in her boots and leaves through the back.

The pizza box is sitting there on the table, but my father says we can't eat anything touched by her dirty hands, so he walks me out into that dark kitchen and he unties me and we go through the cupboards and find mostly boxes of prunes and old cereal. There's nothing in the refrigerator that hasn't already gone bad, so I eat a bowl of cornflakes with water and I'm so hungry, it almost tastes good.

"This is what they call a temporary situation," he says. "I know a way we can live like kings if we play our cards right." He stops for a while and squints at me, like he wants to see inside my head. "We'll be heading for warmer weather. That agreeable with you, boy?"

"Yes, sir, it is."

He seems real thoughtful. "I had a lot of time to plan this out. A lot of time to study people, figure what makes them tick. First thing, we'll get a bus, one of those RV things, a real big one, because it's important to look impressive. Put a name up on the side: The Reverend Kenneth David Kane. Or it might be we'll go with another name, just to be on the safe side. Did you guess I was a man of God, boy, could you tell that by looking at me?"

"Yes, sir," I say. "I mean, no, sir."

"What's that mean, boy?"

"I don't know, sir."

He reaches out and tussles my hair. "You'll learn," he says. "You'll be standing out in front of the bus in a real nice suit. What you do is collect money in a basket. You won't have to steal it because folks will give to a man of God, and what they love to hear about is a bad man who has redeemed himself. I learned how to preach the word to a lot of illiterate convicts, but they were no more ignorant that a lot of other folk. No, sir. We're going to do just fine."

After I finish the cornflakes, he ties me up again.

"This is just a precaution," he says. "Can't take any chances until you see the light. You want to see the light?"

"Yes, sir, I do."

He's grinning at me and he taps himself on the chest and says, "You're looking at it, boy. I am the light, and don't you ever forget it."

He turns on the TV, it hardly comes in at all the screen is so fuzzy, and he keeps switching channels and he's cussing out the old lady for having such a crummy TV. All that's on is Christmas stuff and cartoons and what he wants is the news, to see if we're on it.

"I bet they haven't even missed you," he says. "Kept you down in that cellar like an animal, how would they know?"

We're sitting there waiting for Iggy when the blue lights start flashing bright against the curtains. He grabs me by the neck and shoves me down to the floor and we both lie there. The blue lights go by real slow, and you can see them shining all around the room.

"Might be someone else they're looking for," he says. "A place like this, it could be anybody. Still, you can't be too careful."

When the lights stop flashing, he crawls to the window and looks out.

"There's nothing dumber than a dumb cop," he says. "If they were so smart, they wouldn't be working on Christmas Day, would they?"

"No, sir," I say.

"You hush up, boy, and let me think."

I'm lying there on the floor tied up when Iggy

sneaks in through the back. I know it's him by the draggy way he walks, and the heavy boots.

"Kenny!" he's whispering. "You there?"

"'Course I'm here," he says. "Show yourself."

Iggy comes into the room and his eyes are darting around. At first he's surprised to see me trussed up, then he shrugs and doesn't look at me any more. "Close call," he says. "You see that cop car?"

"I saw it."

"They come right up to my door looking for the boy," he says. "I said, come back with a search warrant, you want to see what I keep under my bed, but I let 'em have a good look from the door, satisfy 'em you weren't there."

"They believe you?"

"Who knows the cops?"

Then my father is sort of dropping his arm around Iggy and giving him a squeeze, and you can see the cold, scared look in Iggy's little eyes, and that wet mouth of his inside his beard. "You turn on me, did you?" my father says. "That how they just happen to come to your place, of all the places in this town?"

Iggy laughs real nervous. "It was that crippled midget kid," he says. "They had him out in the car. It must have been him, Loretta saw him peeking up over the seat."

Freak.

"What midget kid?" my father asks. "You think I'll fall for that?"

Iggy points at me and says, "Ask him does he have a midget friend. The two of 'em stole Loretta's purse, that's how come they know this place. That's the God's honest truth, Kenny."

My father kneels down and looks at me up close. His face doesn't show anything. "Well?" he says. "What's your story?"

"We didn't steal it," I say. "We just brought it back."

"Oh," my father says. "Now *that's* an interesting story. I *like* that story."

Iggy is talking fast, like he can't wait to get rid of the words and leave. "The crippled-up kid belongs to Gwen. Remember Gwen? Her and your wife were pals, that's what Loretta says."

My father puts his hand on Iggy and shoves him down into the old lady's chair. "Never mind about her. It doesn't matter how the cops got on to you, all that matters is they *did*. And now what do we do about it?"

Iggy is scratching at his beard and he starts to say something and my father says, "Shut up and let me think."

Iggy shuts up. Every now and then he sneaks a look at me like he's trying to tell me something with his eyes, but I can't figure out what.

After a while my father says, "First thing, get me a firearm. Something small and functional. Next thing is transportation. I don't care what, as long as it runs. Can you do that for me?"

Iggy says he can, no problem.

"Then do it," my father says. "The quicker the better."

Iggy leaves, walking backwards out of the room. My father lifts me up by the rope and says, "I know you have more sense that to waste your time stealing pocketbooks with a cripple kid. You can't trust a cripple, but I guess you know that now, don't you?"

He shakes the rope.

"Yes, sir, I do."

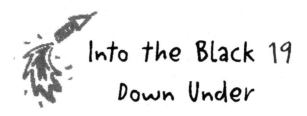

# Into the Black
# Down Under

We have to leave the old lady's place because you never know, the cops might come knocking on each door.

"They're like bugs," my father says. "They're not too smart, but there's lots of them and they keep at it."

On the other side of the alley is this boarded-up building, it used to be part of the Testaments until a fire burned it out, and my father decides we'll hide there until Iggy gets a car for us.

He reaches out and pulls off a big piece of plywood with one hand. The screechy noise the nails make sounds like a cat fight, and the next thing there's a real cat, a black one, that leaps out from behind the plywood. My father jumps so hard, he yanks me to the ground and I bump my head.

"Dumb animal," he says. "Get up now, that's just a scratch, a little blood never hurt a man."

It doesn't hurt, and anyhow I sort of like the taste of salt in my mouth, it makes me feel awake.

"Get in there," he says and then he's pulling me through this old burned-out window and we're inside the building.

Everything is black and wet and dripping except for where snow has come down through holes in the roof. Most of the inside walls are gone, and you can see where the centre beam was chewed by the fire. All the old pipes and wires are hanging down, and everywhere underfoot is broken glass the colour of smoke.

"I used to wonder exactly what Hell looked like," he says. "Now I know."

He finds a place where the stairs go down into the basement and he pulls away the boards and planks. "You should feel right at home," he says. "Cooped up like you were in that cellar hole."

It's so dark he has to use a cigarette lighter, and the flame is so puny, you still can't see to the bottom of the stairs. "You go first," he says. "We can't have both of us on the same step. It might break."

The steps are made of thick wood, but slick and punky soft where the water has been dripping all these years, and I can feel how it sags under my feet. There's a rail that's hard to grab with my hands tied, and the way he's holding up the lighter you might as well keep your eyes closed because it's that dark, you can't see a thing.

I slip and start to fall, and then he's pulling back on the rope and I'm hanging there in the middle of the air with my feet skittering and he's going, "Easy does it, boy. We'll take this one step at a time."

Finally we get to the bottom. There's a little slant of light coming through this narrow cellar window, enough so we can feel our way around all the burned junk that has fallen through the floor.

"The accommodations could be better," he says. "I'll grant you that. Soon as Iggy fixes things, we'll be on our way."

He ties my feet back up and loops the rope tight around this old busted-up boiler that's tipped over, so I can't move or see what's behind me.

"Understand you can't be trusted quite yet," he says. "Once we get on the road, things will be different. You'll get smarter, every mile we put between us and this place."

He rips a piece off my shirt and ties it on my mouth so I can't be shouting, he says, and wake up the neighbourhood. He rubs his hand through my hair again, real gentle. I'm pretty sure there's this sweet smile on his face, although it's so dim you can't be sure. "You just sit tight here a minute," he says. "I have to see a man about a car."

Then he's gliding away, and I hold myself still in case this is a trick and he's really sneaking up behind me to see if I can get my hands loose. Which I can't, they're numb and bloated from the rope cutting into my wrists, and finally I stop trying and just sit there letting my eyes open up in the dark.

I can barely make out that narrow window. Hardly big enough so a cat could slip through, and under it is this big pile of coal slagged up against the foundation wall. Overhead there's creaking with the weight of him moving around, trying to be light on his feet.

I'm listening to him up there and trying to see out that little window when something moves against the light.

I'm pretty sure there's a scratching sound coming from the window, except you can't always believe what you hear in the dark. Then whatever it is goes away and I'm thinking it was probably a cat, or maybe a dog sniffing around. Finally I just keep still, because the more I move, the tighter the rope gets.

Next thing, I hear someone on the steps, these

light feet trying to be real quiet, and then a flashlight comes on and this woman's voice says, "You there, kid?"

Loretta Lee.

I can't say anything because of the gag. All I can do is sort of kick around a little, let her know where I am. You can tell by her shaky, thin voice she's scared of the dark. "Kid? Tell me that's you. Oh, Lord Jesus, what am I *doing* down here?"

Then the beam of that flashlight is hitting me right in the eyes, and she's tripping over stuff trying to get to me. First thing she does is pull the gag off, and I take a deep, deep breath that makes my lungs burn.

"It ain't right," she whispers. "Keeping your own kid tied up, it ain't right. He ain't the man I thought I remembered, that's for sure."

I want to say something, but I'm not sure what and anyhow my mouth is too dry. She's put the flashlight on the floor, aiming up so she can try to untie the rope.

"The man is a genius for knots," she says.

I can feel how her hands are shaking as she's fumbling around. Also I can hear the boards creaking overhead but you can't be sure, it might be just the wind.

Loretta goes, "The plan is, Iggy keeps him busy

**139**

while I get you loose, now isn't that a good plan? There's enough cops up there to start a war, we'll be safe enough if we get out of this godforsaken place."

Her hands are pulling at the rope, nervous and quick, but the knots just keep getting tighter. Finally she gets this idea to cut the rope on the ragged edge of the boiler. "I saw this on the movies once," she whispers. "I forget what movie."

She's working the rope against the sharp edge of that old boiler and sure enough, it cuts through. Just the one cut won't do it, though, and she has to do it twice more before my wrists get loose and I can't really help much because my hands are all numb and swollen.

"Next thing is this piece around your ankles," she says. "I sure can't carry you up out of here. You think you can walk, I get this loose?"

"Yes, ma'am," I say.

That makes her giggle. "My, ain't we got polite all of a sudden," she says. "There, that should about do it."

My feet come loose and I try to stand up and I have to lean some of my weight on her. She goes, "Just a second, Sugar, let me get this flashlight."

She bends over for the flashlight, and then she's making this sound like something is caught in her throat.

Two big hands are squeezing her neck. I see how my father is coming huge out of the dark and he's got his hands around her throat, shoving her back.

"You ignorant creature," he says. "I'll teach you to put your dirty hands on my son."

Loretta can't say anything, she's sinking down on her knees and trying to pull his hands away from her neck, but it's useless, she can't stop him, he's squeezing her dead with his bare hands, and no one can stop him, no one, no one.

# 20 Freak the Mighty Strikes Again

Even a total goon like me knows you can't stop Killer Kane, but I go ahead and try anyhow. My hands are still numbed out and I can hardly walk, so all I can do is sort of fall on top of him and try to shove him loose from her.

I'm going, "Stop! I see you! Daddy, please please stop, you're killing her!"

He just twitches me away. He's made of iron and steel, he's gritting his teeth and squeezing her neck. You can see the white of her eyes, and she's not even trying to get away any more.

I try to get between them and I'm going, "I saw you kill her! I saw you kill Mom! I never forgot, not ever! I know you did it! I *know*!"

It's like I'm trapped underwater or something, so weak and floaty I can't hardly fight him, can't prise his fingers loose from my mother's neck. From Loretta's neck. Because everything is mixed up and he's doing the same thing to Loretta Lee he did to my mom, choking the life out of her, and he's got that same cold killer look because he *wants* her to die, like he wanted Mom to die, and nothing else matters except what he wants.

I'm there in the dark, pushing at him. The light catches her eyes and I can see her looking at me, she's so far away it's like I'm four years old again, peeking out from behind the bedroom door and then running to bang my little fists at him while the light fades from her eyes.

I can't get him loose of her, so all I can do is keep screaming, "I know you killed her! I saw you! I saw you do it! You killed her and I'll never forget, not ever!"

Finally he jerks his head and I can feel him looking at me and then his hands open. Loretta slips away and I can hear her breathing like a broken bird in the cellar dark.

"What?" he says, reaching for me. "What did you say?"

"I saw you do it," I say. "I saw you kill my mother."

"You weren't but four years old," he says, and now his big hands are starting to curl around my neck, except he's holding me soft. I can feel his heart beating, and his cool breath in my face that makes me want to fall asleep. "You can't possibly recall that event," he says. "You think you can, but you can't."

"I can," I say. "I do."

"That's the poison they put in your mind, boy. They brainwashed you into thinking you can remember."

He's pulling me close, holding me soft by the neck, and now I can feel the pulse in his hands.

"They never talk about it," I say. "They don't have to because I can't ever forget it, no matter how much I try."

"No," he says, and his face is so close, I can feel the heat rising off him. "Impossible, you can't."

"You were wearing your brown corduroy trousers," I say, talking so fast, it makes me shake inside. "And the black T-shirt with no sleeves. I tried to stop you but I couldn't and you carried me back into my room and put me to bed and told me I was just dreaming. You locked me in that room and I ran to the window and broke it with my hand and started yelling for someone to come and help Mommy."

My father sighs and says, "Lord, I wish you hadn't done that, boy. It cost me years."

"They caught you, Daddy, and they put you away for ever, except then you fooled them and they let you go."

"I have to clean this up," he says, like he's talking to himself alone. "I have to clean this up and get out of here."

That's when his hands start to tighten hard and fast around my neck. I'm trying to fight him but I'm so small and weak and he's so big and strong, you can't stop him, no one can stop Killer Kane.

He squeezes and squeezes and squeezes.

I'm in this faraway place, falling backwards real slow and dreamy, when I hear a window breaking. Then a small faraway voice is saying, "Put your hands up, villain!" and I really am falling and air is coming back into my lungs so fast, it hurts.

I'm lying there all crumpled and sideways. I can see Freak. He's rolled down through the cellar window into the pile of coal, and he's trying to stand up.

"I'm warning you," he says in that fierce bold way he has.

He's got a squirt gun, one of those big blaster models that holds about a gallon of water.

Killer Kane is looking at me, he's looking at Loretta all crumpled and moaning, he's looking at

Freak. Then he shakes his head and goes, "I know a real gun when I see it, you little monster."

He makes a move, reaching out. Freak scuttles back a little ways but he can't really run and even if he could, there's no place to go.

"This is your partner in crime?" Killer Kane says to me. "I guess maybe you *are* a retard after all."

Freak is pointing the squirt gun right in his face and he says, "Guess what I got for Christmas, Mr Kane? Guess right, because your life depends on it."

Killer Kane doesn't say anything, he's just reaching out real slow because he knows that Freak can't get away.

"This squirt gun," Freak says, "And a chemistry set. That's what I got for Christmas."

Killer Kane just looks at the squirt gun. He shakes his head, like who are you kidding?

"Sulphuric acid," Freak says, raising up the gun and sighting along the barrel. "Good old reliable $H_2SO_4$, an oily, colourless, corrosive liquid used in dyes, paints, explosives, and many chemical experiments."

Killer Kane says, "You're lying, kid, you can't fool me."

That's when Freak squeezes the trigger and sprays him right in the eyes.

Then Killer Kane is screaming in this high, scared voice. His hands are scrubbing at his eyes and it's like that scream wakes me up, because the next thing I know I've got Freak in my arms and I'm running through the dark for the stairs, running as fast as I can on feet I can't even feel.

"Go!" Freak is yelling. "He's right behind you, go!"

I can't look back but I can feel him, feel the icy-cold of him on the back of my neck, and the hands reaching blind to grab me and then I'm going up the stairs, just flying.

The steps are breaking under my feet and he's howling in rage behind me, his hands are scrabbling at my ankles and for just a second he has me.

I kick loose and then we're up on the ground floor, bursting out of the cellar hole. I can see daylight coming through the boarded-up plywood and I cover Freak with my arms and just dive through that plywood, *wham.*

The sunlight blinds me and we're skitter-rolling though the clean, cold snow.

Hands are grabbing me, and I'm fighting to get away.

"Easy!" a voice says. "Take it easy, kid, you're okay!"

Iggy Lee. He's looking down at me with red eyes

and you can see where he's been chewing at his beard. I'm sitting there in the snow squinting up at Iggy and all these cops, there must be a million cops, and Freak is laughing like a maniac and saying, "It worked! He fell for it! Soap and vinegar and curry powder! It worked like a charm!"

I don't understand what he's talking about right then, it's only later I figure out there wasn't any real acid in the squirt gun, it was soap and vinegar and curry powder that made Killer Kane think his eyes were burning up – Killer Kane, who is still rubbing frantic at his eyes and begging for help when they put the handcuffs on him and shove him into the back of the police van.

All I've got room to think about is poor Loretta. That's what I'm telling the cops, that she's down there in the cellar. I'm afraid that no one is listening but they must be, because right away they're bringing her up out of the cellar and Iggy is running to her and crying out her name.

"She's still breathing," somebody says.

Then Gram is shoving through the crowd of cops and Grim is right behind her, and Gwen is there, too, and everybody is making a big, sloppy fuss, especially Gram, who's hugging me so tight I can't hardly breathe.

The Fair Gwen is hugging Freak and she's saying, "I told you to stay in that car, didn't I? Didn't I?"

Freak, he's looking over her shoulder at me looking over Gram's shoulder, and he gives me the thumbs-up sign as she carries him away.

"Freak the Mighty!" he says. "Freak the Mighty strikes again!"

# 21 The Accident of Nature

We all of us had to go down to the police station, of course, where they took a bunch of pictures of the bruises on my neck, and then they insisted I needed X-rays and so we had to go over to the hospital and get *that* done and then go back to the police station again, which wore on my nerves almost as much as being kidnapped.

Grim, the second time we go to the cops, he's sitting there in this room with me waiting, and he says, "I can't tell you what it felt like, coming up out of the basement and seeing that double track of footprints in the snow. I knew it was him, I just knew in my heart."

He kept insisting that Gram go home, which she finally did, because we were there at the police station for hours more, me telling all about it over and over, until I thought I would faint dead away if just one more person asked me what happened after I woke up in the dark and was stolen from my own bed.

Grim, he just keeps patting me on the arm and saying, "This is important, Max. Maybe this time they'll lock him up for good."

That's what everybody keeps saying, that this time they've got Killer Kane where they want him, in violation of parole, in violation of a restraining order, abduction of a minor, and two counts of attempted murder, me and the Heroic Biker Babe, which is what the papers took to calling Loretta Lee.

The word is she's hurt pretty bad because he cracked a bone in her neck, but she'll be okay in the long run. Iggy, when I saw him that time in the hospital waiting, he was chewing a hole right through his beard he was so worried, and it made me think he wasn't such a bad dude after all.

It all goes to show, like Grim says, that you can't always judge a book by the cover.

* * *

It turns out to be a pretty weird Christmas vacation, as you might imagine, and Gram keeps fussing at me and won't let me sleep in the cellar.

"I don't care if he *is* under lock and key," she says.

Grim, he says please humour the woman, she's worried about to death, and so I sleep upstairs on the foldout and at night Gram keeps checking to see I'm there. Which is a pain, but she can't help herself, and anyhow I'm just as glad not to be alone in the down under.

Freak, well, the Fair Gwen just about threw a fit when she got him home, because of him disobeying a direct order and sneaking away to rescue me, but after a while she calms down and all she does is just look at him and shake her head.

"What am I going to do with you?" she asks.

"Put me up for adoption," he says. "I want to go live with the Waltons."

He means the TV show that keeps repeating, and of course he's teasing her, but the Fair Gwen is not amused.

"No more crazy adventures, or dangerous quests, young man. You have to be careful," she keeps saying. "Extra careful."

She means the trouble he has sometimes catching his breath, because of the way his insides keep growing faster than his outside, which hasn't really grown at all.

Freak goes into the medical research place every few months now, which he says is a real pain, not that it actually hurts.

"Dr. Spivak says my unique status as a marvel of genetic aberration makes me an object of intense curiosity," he says in that lofty way of his. "Specialists from the world over are familiar with my case."

"What about the secret operation?" I ask when the Fair Gwen can't hear us. "The one where you'll get a robot body?"

Freak gets this very cool, scientific look on his face, and he always says the same thing: "The bionic research continues, my friend. The work goes on."

I don't know why I keep asking, because it gives me the creeps. You'd think I could be as cool as Freak about the idea, because it's him that's going to get a new bionic body, but just thinking about it makes me want to jump up and run around.

I keep telling Gram that when Freak is in the hospital for his tests I shouldn't have to go to school, because we're like a team, but she won't buy it.

"I know Kevin has been a great help to you," she says. "But you've got a brain of your own, haven't you dear?"

Yeah, right.

The other thing about school that's different after Christmas vacation is how jealous everybody is that we got our pictures in the paper and on the local TV. Mrs. Donelli in English calls us "the dynamic duo" and she put a cutout picture from the paper up on the bulletin board. Wouldn't you know some goon put moustaches on us the very first day.

Freak says he looks cool with a moustache and he can't wait to grow one, and he makes Mrs. Donelli leave the picture up. Me, I'd just as soon forget about the whole thing. I really hate the idea of having to testify at the trial and tell what really happened, but everybody says I have to, if I want him locked up for the rest of his life. Which I do, especially after what he tried to do to poor Loretta, who was only trying to help.

"They can't make you if you don't want to," Freak says. "A son doesn't have to testify against his father."

"Grim thinks it will do me good. Plus he's really worried he'll get off again, or fool the jury by quoting from the Bible."

"Grim worries too much," Freak says. "*Everybody* worries too much."

The way it finally turns out with Killer Kane, Freak is right. Because just before the trial is supposed to start, and I've got my fingernails chewed down to the second knuckle, Grim gets this telephone call that makes him punch his fist in the air and go, "Yes! Yes!"

What happened, they made a deal and Killer Kane pleaded guilty, which means he has to serve out the rest of his original sentence plus ten more years.

"He'll be an old man when he gets out," Grim says. "He'll be older than me."

That should make me happy, but instead I feel really weird and worried, and Grim, who still thinks he knows everything, says I just have to get used to the idea.

"The man is an accident of nature," he says. "All you got from him is your looks and your size. You've got your mother's heart, and that's what counts."

The weird thing I keep thinking about, what if something happens when I get older and I turn out to be another accident of nature?

Grim sees me thinking about that one night just before bed, and he sits on the end of the foldout and he says, "Things will make a lot more sense when you finish growing up, Maxwell. Now sleep tight and don't let the bedbugs bite."

Grim means well, I know that, but sometimes he says the numbest things. Because it's growing up that worries me.

# 22 Remembering Is Just an Invention of the Mind

"Spring has sprung," Freak says. "And so are we."

This is the day school gets out, and we're taking the long way home. By now I've been carrying him around on my shoulders for almost a year. We call it walking high, and even if we haven't been going on any dangerous quests lately, so the Fair Gwen won't have to throw a fit, Freak hasn't exactly given up on slaying dragons.

"The world is really and truly green all over," he says. "Do you remember what it used to be like, back in the Ice Age, when the glaciers covered the earth and the sabre-toothed tiger roamed the frozen night?"

"Uh, no," I say. "How could I remember that? I wasn't even born."

"Don't be a pinhead," he says. "Remembering is just an invention of the mind."

I go, "What's that supposed to mean?"

"It means that if you want to, you can remember anything, whether it happened or not. Like I can remember what it was like in the Ice Age. I kept trying to invent stuff – the wheel, central heating, indoor plumbing – but the Neanderthals were happy with just a campfire and a fur coat."

If you guessed that Freak has been reading a book about the Ice Age, you're right. He's been seeing a sabre-toothed tiger behind every bush, except that so far, all of them have turned out to be stray cats, or once it was this skunk and it's a good thing I can run fast or we'd have to soak in tomato juice, which is the only way to get rid of the stink.

"Inventing electricity would be tough," he says, "without copper wire and magnets, but I could handle inventing a compass – all you have to do is rub the needle. That way everybody could head south and get away from the glaciers."

"First you need to invent a time machine," I say. "So you can go back there and give all the cavemen a hard time about indoor plumbing."

Freak goes, "You don't need a time machine if you know how to remember."

Which is something I'll always remember, him saying that and me trying to figure it out.

* * *

Freak's birthday is a couple of days after school gets out, and the Fair Gwen has already made it clear he's not getting a ride on the space shuttle.

"Thirteen is supposed to be extra special," he says. "The least you could do is get my name on the list. Or how about a linear accelerator, just a small one so I can split a few atoms?"

The Fair Gwen goes, "I suppose this means you're going to be an obnoxious teenager."

The deal is, this is really two birthdays for the price of one, because Freak the Mighty is almost a year old.

"Talk about a prodigy," Freak says. "One year old and already he's on his way to ninth grade."

The Fair Gwen just rolls her eyes when we talk like that. Freak says we can't expect her to understand, because you can't *really* get what it means to be Freak the Mighty unless you *are* Freak the Mighty.

Anyhow, the party is just a family affair because Freak isn't supposed to get overexcited, which is like saying the moon isn't supposed to go around the earth.

"Last year I got the ornithopter," he says. "This year, why not a helicopter? A real one, though, you can't expect a teenager to play with toys."

"Why not a jet plane?" the Fair Gwen says.

"Cool," Freak says. "A Learjet."

What he's really getting, and I've been sworn to secrecy, is this new computer, the one he's been drooling over in his computer magazines. It comes with a modem, which means if he has to stay home for some reason, he can go to school over the telephone. The idea is I'd be there in the classroom with a matching computer. The only problem, I don't know squid about computers.

"You'll learn," the Fair Gwen says. "Kevin will teach you."

"But why should he have to stay home?" I ask her.

We're out in the kitchen and she and Gram are frosting the cakes and Freak is hanging out in the living room, acting like he intends to have a party every day for the rest of his life.

"Maybe he won't have to stay home," the Fair Gwen says, and she and Gram kind of lock eyeballs for a second, that secret code that mothers have. "This is just in case, Max."

"I think maybe he already guessed about the computer," I say. "That's why he's jerking your chain about the space shuttle ride and Learjets."

"I'm not surprised," the Fair Gwen says. "You can't keep anything from Kevin."

159

Freak hardly touches his supper, he says he's saving his appetite for the cake, and finally we're all done eating except for Grim, who keeps rubbing his belly and rolling his eyes and telling the Fair Gwen what a genius she is with fresh peas and new potatoes and salmon and he'll have just a smidgeon more, thanks, and finally Gram clears her throat and smiles and Grim has to apologize for being such a pig.

The funny thing is, when at last they do bring out the cake, Freak asks me to flame out the candles while he makes the wish, and then he doesn't even touch his piece, he just sort of pushes it around the plate. I figure he's so excited about getting the new computer that he's lost his appetite. Not that he's letting on he doesn't feel good, he's acting just as wise and smart-mouthed as ever.

"I should have asked for earplugs," he says when we're done singing "Happy Birthday". "You better check the glassware for cracks."

"Hush up," the Fair Gwen says, "or we'll give you another chorus."

When she brings out the computer he acts so surprised and happy, maybe he really *is* surprised. Right away he wants to turn it on and show off what a brain he is, and because it's his birthday we all have to sit there and admire him and go, "Amazing," and "Fantastic," and "Kevin, how did you know that?" and so on.

He's showing Grim how to play 3-D chess, and just watching that makes me dizzy, so after a while I go out to the kitchen and help clean up, which is something I'm good at.

"Maxwell never breaks a dish," Gram is saying. "He's very sure-handed for someone so large."

We're almost done putting stuff away and wiping the counter when Grim shouts from the other room.

All he says is, "Kevin!" but we can tell right away that something is wrong.

We run in and Freak is leaning back in his chair making this wheezing sound, panting real fast, and his eyelids are flickering.

"He's having a seizure," Grim says. "Call an ambulance."

The Fair Gwen is already on the phone.

I run out in the street and start waving my arms and jumping up and down so they'll know where to stop, and I keep running back in the house to check on things, but the Fair Gwen says there's nothing we can do except wait.

# 23 The Empty Book

They won't let me visit him the first day, and Gram says I'll just have to be patient and let the doctors do their business, but I can't stand just sitting around so I decide to walk over to the hospital, which Grim says is miles and miles, but suit myself.

I know how to get there because Freak and I went yonder that way once so he could show me the medical research building. It's not the same, though, without Freak along to turn the houses into castles and the swimming pools into moats.

All I keep thinking is, what a gyp it is to have to go into the hospital on your birthday.

Finally I get there and I see the Fair Gwen's car in the visitor parking lot, but Grim says I should leave her alone and let her tend to her son, so what I do is go around back to the medical research building and find this stupid little tree I can sit under.

I have that old ornithopter bird with me and I'm winding it up and flying it around. Figuring maybe Freak will get a chance to look out the window and see it flittering by, that's my plan, and I'm under that puny little tree messing with the bird until this guy mowing the lawn makes me move. So I wander around to the front of the hospital and that's when the Fair Gwen finds me.

"Maxwell!" she says, and she gives me this great big hug. A wet hug because she's been crying. "Max, we've been looking all over for you. Kevin wants to see you. He's making quite a fuss about it and Dr. Spivak says it's okay, but just for a few minutes."

So the Fair Gwen takes me inside, and I figure we're heading for the medical research building, but instead we go into the regular hospital.

"He's in the ICU," she says.

"So they're taking really good care of him?"

"They're doing their best, Max," she says.

The intensive care unit is this place where there are so many nurses, you can't hardly turn around without bumping into one, which I do as soon as we get there. Every patient gets a room alone, and there's all this electronic gear the Fair Gwen says is called "telemetry", which means when Freak sneezes, the nurses know about it before he can wipe his nose.

I'm not scared at all until I actually go into his room and see how small he looks on the bed. They've got him sitting up with all these tubes going into his arms and up his nose and Dr. Spivak is guarding him, she won't let me come too close.

"I thought no visitors was the best policy for now," Dr. Spivak says. "But what Kevin wants, Kevin gets."

Dr. Spivak is this small woman with short red hair and a real stern face, and it's like she's mad because Freak wants to see me, or because I'll break some of her precious equipment.

"That will be all," Freak says to her. "You are dismissed."

The thing is, his voice sounds funny. Not just faint and weak, but kind of whistley. Only when I get closer do I see he's got this weird little plastic button stuck in his neck.

"It's called a tracheotomy," he says, holding his finger against the button, which stops the whistling noise. "Standard procedure to facilitate breathing."

"Does it hurt?"

"No way," he says. "I think it's cool. Listen to this."

Then he plays with his finger against the button,

making his throat whistle a tune, which he says is the theme from *Star Trek*, although you can hardly recognize it.

"So when do you come home?" I ask.

Freak can't move much the way they've got him set up in the bed, so he sort of shakes his eyes instead of his head. "I'm not coming home," he says. "Not in my present manifestation."

I go, "What?"

"The Bionic Unit is on red alert," he says. "Tonight they'll take me down there for my special operation. The next time you see me, I'll be new and improved."

"I'm scared," I say.

"Don't be a moron," he says. "You're not the one having surgery."

"I still wish they wouldn't."

"Don't argue with me," he says.

I have to lean close to hear him because his voice is so small and whispery.

He goes, "If you argue with me, I'll get upset and they can tell on the telemetry. Then *you'll* get in trouble."

So I just stand there like a lump and don't say anything for a while. I put the ornithopter on the foot of the bed, but I don't think he notices.

"See that book on the table?"

He can't point, but I see the book on the table.

"Open it," he says.

The book reminds me of the dictionary he gave me for Christmas, except when I open it, all the pages are blank.

"That's for you," he says. "I want you to fill it up with our adventures."

"Huh?"

"Write it down, dummy. I was going to do it, but now it looks like I'll be busy getting used to my new bionic body. It'll probably take me weeks just learning how to walk with long legs."

I put the book down.

"You're the one with the brain," I say. "I'm the long legs."

"Don't get me upset," he warns. "I won't have the time, so you'll have to do it. Just write it all down like you're talking. Put in all the fun we had, the cool things we did. Our adventures."

"But you *know* I can't write, Kevin."

"It's all in your head, Max, everything you can remember. Just tell the story of Freak the Mighty, no big deal."

I pick the book back up but I don't say anything more about how hopeless it is, me trying to write stuff down, because I don't want to set off the telemetry. He does that himself about a minute later when he starts to cough and before I can say anything, the room is swarming with nurses and Dr. Spivak is telling me I have to leave.

"Out this second, young man, and let us do our jobs."

They let me wait outside the ICU with the Fair Gwen, who is just standing there at the window wringing her hands and not saying anything, and then finally they come out and say he's okay, it was just a bad spell, that they have him stabilized.

A while later Gram comes into the hospital and she drives me home. Nobody talks much at supper that night, except when Grim opens his big mouth and says, "Poor Gwen looks like she's in terrible pain."

I go, "Poor Gwen? She's not the one having the special operation."

Grim and Gram just look at each other like they can't believe I'm so dumb, and finally Gram says, "Maxwell, dear, make an effort to eat your vegetables."

That night I put the empty book in the pyramid box for safekeeping, and for good luck.

# 24 The Return of Kicker

The deal is, I'm not supposed to bother anybody at the hospital. Yeah, right, like me being there is going to screw things up. The way everybody is acting around here, you're supposed to shut up and not do anything but wait, which makes me crazy.

So early the next morning when Grim is still snoring loud enough to rattle the windowpanes, I get up and sneak out of the house. The way I figure, I can check on Freak and be back in time for breakfast, no harm done.

It doesn't work out like that, to say the least.

The sun is just coming over the millpond and there's this spooky mist on the water. You can hear all the frogs making a racket under the lily pads and the mosquitoes sound like bullets whizzing by and I have to kind of slap and run until I get clear of that smelly old pond.

Moving fast, like the sun is chasing my heels, I'm running down this long faint shadow of me that stretches out ahead, you can't ever catch up with it.

I'm thinking with my feet, like the rest of me is still asleep.

Not that I'm completely alone. There's this one old guy, he's actually out cutting his lawn, he's got these headlights rigged up on his rider mower, and he's wearing pyjamas, too, like it's normal, everybody does it.

When I get to the hospital the streetlights are just starting to click off. The lobby is empty and there's nobody at the desk to tell me I can't be visiting patients at the crack of dawn.

There are plenty of nurses in the ICU, though, and they see me coming. This one woman turns right out from behind the telemetry station and she's got her hands up to her mouth and I'm pretty sure she's trying to shush me, even though I'm not making any noise.

She's not telling me to be quiet, though, she's saying, "Oh, my God, you must be Maxwell," even though she's never seen me before in her life.

I go, "Is Kevin back yet?"

"Oh dear, oh dear," she says.

"Is he going to be okay?"

"Oh dear," she says. "Oh dear."

Now more nurses are coming out of the ICU. One of them is the one I accidentally bumped into yesterday and when she sees me, she goes, "Better page Dr. Spivak, Kevin was her patient."

That's when I notice that some of the nurses are crying and looking at me strange and all of a sudden I just go nuts.

Just go nuts.

I'm saying, "No way! No way!" and this nurse is trying to throw a hug on me and I push her away.

Then I'm running down the hall and it's like I'm Kicker again, ready to just blast anybody who dares touch me, and I have to keep running, I'm skidding around the corners and bumping into walls and no one can touch me even if they're brave enough to try, I just keep running and running until I get to these glass doors that say MEDICAL RESEARCH.

The doors are locked and it's dark inside.

Behind me people are shouting to call the guards, and I punch my hand right through the glass and I'm inside, skidding over the broken glass through the dark, and I keep going until I come to this other set of doors.

NO ADMITTANCE

No glass this time, they're solid so I can't punch through, and I'm kicking and kicking and slamming into the doors, and that's when all the hospital cops catch up with me.

A bunch of them jump on me and I keep going, running around in circles like an accident of nature until finally there are so many of them on me, I can't stand up any more.

They're putting handcuffs on my wrists and my ankles and they're sitting on me and going, "We'll have to medicate him," and this one cop says, "With what, an elephant gun?"

That's how Dr. Spivak finds me, covered with cops. She's this worried face leaning down. Her eyes are red and blurry and she's saying, "I'm sorry, Maxwell, we did our best. Better let me bandage up that hand, you're bleeding."

"He believed you," I say. "You said you could give him a new body and he believed you."

"What are you talking about?"

"The special operation," I say. "The Bionics Unit."

Dr. Spivak makes the cops let me up and says she'll be responsible, but they leave the handcuffs on me just in case, and the cop who was talking about needing an elephant gun has this nightstick out and he's ready to bop me if I make a move.

Dr. Spivak sighs and says, "Somebody get me a coffee, please," and then she looks at me and goes, "you'd better tell me all about it."

So while she's bandaging up my hand, I tell her about how Freak has been coming to the medical research lab every few months to get fitted for his new bionic body, and Dr. Spivak's face goes soft and she nods to herself and says, "Well, that explains it."

"It was all a lie, wasn't it?" I say. "You were just telling him that so he wouldn't be scared."

"You know better than that, Maxwell. You couldn't lie to Kevin. I tried a little fib on him when he was about seven years old, because I didn't think a child could handle the whole truth, and you know what he did? He looked his disease up in a medical dictionary."

That's when I know she's telling the truth. Freak and his dictionary.

"Kevin knew from a very young age that he wasn't going to have a very long life," she says. "He knew it was just a matter of time."

"So he was lying about getting a robot body?"

Dr. Spivak is shaking her head. "I don't think it was a lie, Maxwell, do you? I think he needed something to hope for and so he invented this

172

rather remarkable fantasy you describe. Everybody needs something to hope for. Don't call it a lie. Kevin wasn't a liar."

"No," I say. "But what happened to him really?"

"I could tell you all the medical terminology," she says. "But what finally happened is his heart just got too big for his body."

There was talk about arresting me for busting up the hospital – the cop with the nightstick was in favour – but finally they released me into the custody of Grim.

On the way home he goes, "Do you want to talk about it?"

"Just leave me alone," I say.

"You got it," he says.

# 25 What Loretta Said

That was a year ago.

I hid in the down under for days and days and kept the door closed, which is why I missed the funeral and the Fair Gwen going away. Gram told me about it afterwards, how she couldn't stand to live in the house with Kevin gone, and who could blame her?

Grim threatened to unscrew my bedroom door but he never did, he just kept saying I should come out for Gram's sake, and sometimes *she'd* come down and say I should come out for Grim's sake, and so on and so forth until finally I gave up and came out.

I don't know if this makes sense, but for a long time I felt like I was a balloon and somebody had let the air out of me. I didn't care if I ever got the air back, because what does it really matter if we're all going to die in the end?

That's how down I was feeling, and sorry for myself. Grim tried to tell me it isn't how long you've got that matters, it's what you do with the time you have, but that sounded so lame and puny next to Freak dying that I just didn't want to hear it.

This one day just before school was supposed to start I was moping around the back yard and thinking again how pointless and stupid everything was and Grim comes over and he says, "You know what? Most of us go all the way through life and we never have a friend like Kevin. So maybe you should count yourself lucky."

"Yeah, right," I say.

"Suit yourself," he says. "But let's get one thing straight. You're going back to school if I have to hitch a rope to the bumper and drag you there, is that clear?"

So I went and I hated every minute of it, and I especially hated how people kept feeling sorry for me, as if it was me who died.

Finally one time even Tony D. came up to me and said it was a shame what happened, and I could see that he really meant it, and I just blew up and told him if he ever felt sorry for me again, I'd put him headfirst in the millpond and pound him down into the mud like a fence post. So we're enemies again, which is just the way I like it.

Not too long after that – this was winter by then – I saw Loretta Lee in the street. She still had on the neck brace and you could smell booze on her breath, but what do you expect, a miracle just because she lost her head and acted good for a couple of minutes?

Anyhow, Loretta sees me and she says, "Did you hear about Gwen? She's in California and she's got this new boyfriend. His name is Rick and they're crazy about each other, ain't that good news?"

"I guess so."

"Take it from me," she says, "it is. So what are you doing these days?"

"Nothing."

She gives me this long look and she goes, "Nothing is a drag, kid. Think about it."

I thought about it all the way home.

That night I pulled the pyramid box from under the bed and got the empty book out of the pyramid and I'm thinking, who are you kidding, Maxwell Kane, you haven't got a brain, and that's the truth, the whole truth, the unvanquished truth is how Freak would say it.

So I wrote the unvanquished truth stuff down and then kept on going, for months and months, until it was spring again, and the world was really and truly green all over. By the time we got here, which I guess should be the end, I'm feeling okay about remembering things. And now that I've written a book who knows, I might even read a few.

No big deal.

# FREAK'S DICTIONARY

## A

AARDVARK, a silly-looking creature that eats ants

AARGH, what the aardvark says when it eats ants

ABACUS, a finger-powered computer

ABSCISSA, the horizontal truth

ALGORITHM, maths with a rock-'n'-rock beat

ALIMENTARY, what Sherlock Holmes said to Dr. Watson about where the food disappeared

ALLEGORY, a peculiar kind of story that's often pretty gory

ARCHETYPE, what Max sees when he dreams of architects

ARITHMETIC, inventing with numbers

ARMOUR, a robotlike suit worn by knights of old

## B

BIG LIE, ignorance is bliss

BIONIC, a way to improve on the human condition

BLOVIATE, to expel hot air in the form of words

BOATS, shoes big enough to fit Maxwell Kane

BOOK, a four-letter word for truth serum
BRAIN, a muscle that improves with exercise
BUTTHEAD, one who can sneeze a hot dog through his nose

## C

CAMOUFLAGE, how a camel blends into the desert
CIGARETTE, something that should be obscene, not smoked
COPACETIC, the fair Gwen's word for "everything is cool"
CRETIN, another name for Blade
CRITTERS, small, irritating children, also known as rug rats

## D

DEMEANOUR, the meaner your face, the worse your demeanour
DICTIONARY, a source of knowledge, fun, and rude jokes
DOWN UNDER, a land far away in Maxwell's basement
DYAD, another word for Max and Kevin
DYNE, unit of energy needed to move a gram one centimetre per second per second

## E

EDIFICATION, education that tastes good
ERG, a measure of energy equal to one dyne per centimetre
EXCALIBUR, a sword with magic powers

# F

FEALTY, loyalty with an "f"

FOLDEROL, Grim's word for nonsense

FOOD, fuel for humans, preferably so-called junk or UFO

FOOZLE, to make a stupid mistake

FORNAX, a cool-sounding constellation

FORMICIDAE, a type of insect never found in Kevin's pants

FURFURACEOUS, covered with dandruff

# G

GADZOOKS, what Grim says when surprised

GALAHAD, son of Lancelot, finder of the Holy Grail

GOON, a four-letter word for Max in a bad mood

GRAM, a sweet lady of light

GRIM, a gentleman of the old school, before they tore
it down

GRUEL, whatever you want more of

# H

HABERDASHER, a person who chases after windblown hats

HAIKU, versification
　　　by the quantum mechanic
　　　means numberless sum

HAMMERHEAD, a know-it-all

HERSTORY, the past, from the female point of view

HIEROGLYPHICS, Max's handwriting

HISTORY, the past, from the male point of view
HOLUS-BOLUS, all at once
HUMAN, an improbable, imperfect creature


# I

IAPETUS, a cool-sounding moon that orbits Saturn
ICARUS, a high-flyer, as in "to do an icarus"
ICHTHYOLOGY, the study of icky foods, for instance fish
IDEA, a seed you plant in your head
IGNEOUS, too hot to eat
INCANDESCENT, an excellent idea
INTERGALACTIC, out of this world


# J

JABBAWOCKY, the language of Jabba the Hut
JILLION, millions and millions
JITTERBUG, a nervous cockroach
JOCULAR, amusingly athletic
JOCULARITY, a joke made by a jock
JOULE, a measure of energy equal to ten million ergs
JURASSIC, cool, excellent, what the fair Gwen calls
"far-out"


# K

KAZOO, a place where weird-sounding musical instruments
are kept in cages

KEVIN, a unit of measurement equal to 70 centimetres
KINETICS, the study of small families
KNIGHT, rhymes with bright and fight and right
KONG, another word for falling down

# L

LACRIMATION, an emotional display to be avoided
LAGOON, a French gangster
LANCELOT, King Arthur's bravest knight
LEXICOGRAPHY, what Webster invented, Kevin perfected
LIBRARY, where they keep the truth serum, and the magic
carpets
LIFTOFF, what happens when you open a book
LIMERICK, a mighty dude called Max,
        saved his pal from bad attacks,
        then they conquered the world,
        with banner unfurled,
        and time left over for snacks

# M

MAGNESIUM, the white sparkles in skyrockets
MASSIVES, fat heads who assume that television tells the
truth
MATHS, you have nothing to fear but maths itself
MAX, a unit of measurement equal to 190 centimetres and
still growing

MEGAPOD, Max's shoe size
MIDGET, a word used by people with small minds
MUCIFEROUS, any disgusting food, as in muciferous tapioca

# N

NANOSECOND, one-billionth of a second
NEANDERTHALS, what we all were before plumbing was invented
NICOTINE, a toxic waste of time
NONILLION, millions of septillions

# O

OBFUSCATE, a needlessly confusing word for needlessly confusing
OBSTINATE, Kevin when he knows he's right
ODORIFEROUS, sneaker perfume
OLFACTORY, where they manufacture smells
ORNITHOPTER, a big word for mechanical bird

# P

PERCIVALE, a knight who saw the Holy Grail
PHYSICS, what matters to energy
POSTULATE, when you presume to assume
POTASSIUM CHLORATE, the womp in a skyrocket
POTASSIUM NITRATE, the bang in a skyrocket
PRIMORDIAL, the good old days

PRIMORDIAL OOZE, boring conversation about the good old days

## Q

QUADRILLION, more than a billion, less than a quintillion
QUANTIC, more than enough, as in "quantic amounts of carrots"
QUANTUM, imaginary sums of impossible numbers
QUEST, an adventure in which you have to use your imagination
QUINTILLION, more than a quadrillion, less than a septillion

## R

READING, beaming up into books
RELATIVITY, the study of mysterious relatives
ROBOTICS, the science of designing and building robots
ROBOT, a mechanical entity, sometimes endowed with human characteristics
ROUND TABLE, where King Arthur passes out the snack food

## S

SAUROPOD, a vegan
SEISMIC, so exciting it makes you vibrate
SEPTILLION, billions of billions
SPASTIC, how the fair Gwen talks when she's nervous
STRONTIUM NITRATE, the blue in a skyrocket

## T

TELEMETRY, how to make nurses jump every time you sneeze

TELEVISION, the opiate of the massives

TELLURIAN, another word for earthling

TIME MACHINE, your imagination

TRACHEOTOMY, a unique method of whistling the "Star Trek" theme

TROGLODYTE, one who hates books

TUBILIFEROUS, splendid, close to perfect

## U

UFOLOGY, see under food; the study of the Unidentified Frying Objects

UNICORN, a horse who makes a point

## V

VAMOOSE, what you say to a moose when you want it to leave

VANQUISH, to defeat in battle, preferably with dragons

VEGAN, a human sauropod

VISCOUS, a thick, vicious liquid

## W

WATT, a measure of electricity equal to one joule per second

WRITING, talking on paper

## X

XYLOID, another word for blockhead

## Y

YONDER, a place that always lies over the next horizon

## Z

ZAG, what you do after you zig

ZED, a Z in England

ZEST, the zing in orange

ZIG, what you do before you zag

ZING, what you taste when you bite into an orange

ZIT, adolescent eruption, not to be confused with teenage volcano

ZOO, an eighth-grade English class

RODMAN PHILBRICK has been writing since the age of sixteen. He had published more than a dozen novels for adults before the publication of his first book for younger readers, *Freak the Mighty*. Since then, he has won numerous awards and honours, including the prestigious California Young Reader Medal, the Arizona Young Readers' Award and the New York State "Charlotte" Award.

"It was my privilege to know an extraordinary young man who lived with a rare spinal condition that meant he would never be much more than three feet tall," Philbrick says. "Despite severe medical problems and an uncertain future, my brilliant young friend faced life with unconquerable spirits. His remarkable personality inspired me to write an entirely fictional story, called *Freak the Mighty*."

*Freak the Mighty* has been translated into many languages and was made into the feature film, *The Mighty*, starring Sharon Stone, with theme music by Sting.

Rod and his wife divide their time between Maine and the Florida Keys, USA.

# About the Author
## In his own words

"I started writing stories in sixth grade. But writing wasn't cool, like being good at sports, or being part of the in crowd, or winning fights in the playground. It wasn't a 'normal' activity, and like most kids that age, I desperately wanted to be 'normal'. So writing became my secret life.

"At the age of sixteen I completed a novel – a book-length series of stories about two characters. The narrator is a boy who admires his best friend, who is a kind of genius, and the gifted friend eventually dies a tragic death. The two buddies hang out in the basement and share a series of adventures. It was rejected. No surprise, actually, because I wasn't like the genius kid I was writing about. The book simply wasn't good enough to be published.

"Eleven years after I finished that first novel, I was still unpublished. But I was determined to make my living as an author. So I kept writing. In the meantime, I worked a variety of labouring jobs – longshoreman, carpenter, boat builder – and started a couple of businesses that went nowhere. Finally, I found a publisher for my genre novels, which were mostly mysteries and thrillers for grown-ups.

"After I had written more than a dozen adult genre novels, an editor I knew in New York asked me to write a mystery for young adults. I said I wasn't interested; but on my way home to Maine, I heard a voice in my head. It was the voice of Maxwell Kane, and he wanted to tell me the story of his little genius buddy. The voice in my head became *Freak the Mighty*, and much of it came directly out of the novel I had written as a sixteen year old.

"That insistent kid voice in my head has helped me reinvent myself as a writer. That voice is still talking, demanding that I write down his story. It was that voice that made me realize that I do, indeed, have stories to tell for sixth, seventh, and eighth graders – stories about spirited kids who find a way to triumph over adversity.

"How do you keep the voice coming? A good memory helps. I vividly remember my sixth-grade classroom. I remember what it smelled like, where I sat, what I could see out the window, and how I felt about things. Peel away my decrepit middle-aged exterior, and an important part of me is still twelve years old. It helps me when I sit down to write stories for kids.

"And here's where the Young Adult author gets the big payoff. If a kid enjoys a book, she or he *really* enjoys it. Kids read uncritically, in the best sense of the word. They care about how the story makes them feel. If a story makes any impression at all, they write to the author. Let me tell you, those letters are just wonderful. The vast majority of young readers speak to you straight from the heart. *I liked this part, it made me laugh. I liked that part, it made me cry.* That was the wonderful surprise, the something extra I never expected in my secret life as a writer. Letters from kids I've never met, but who speak to me with a clarity and personality that makes them leap from the page.

"I love getting these fresh, wonder-filled messages from kids. As a writer I'm convinced that encouraging children to write fiction, to hook into that marvellous machine called the imagination, has to be good for everyone. It's good for the teachers who see students bloom into writers under their tutelage. It's good for the kids, who learn that they can work the same kind of magic they find in books. It's good for all of us, because soon these kids are going to emerge as the next generation of authors – and there won't have to be any 'secret' about it."

# An interview with
# Rodman Philbrick

**Out of all the characters in your books, is there one that has become your favorite? If so, who?**
The character that is my favorite is always the character I'm writing about right now. But, to be honest, I have great affection for Maxwell Kane, because he's the one who got me into writing books for younger readers. He was the first character I wrote about.

**What medical disorder does Freak suffer from?**
Freak's illness is called "morquio syndrome." It's a fairly rare form of dwarfism, but there are a number of kids in the USA who were born with it. I've heard from a few. It may be a coincidence, but the morquio kids I know are all highly intelligent and very creative.

**Why did you decide to have Freak die in the book?**
I didn't decide to have Freak die. The character Kevin

was based on died in real life. And I didn't think that I could change reality and remain true to the story. The fact is, if the boy who inspired the character of Kevin hadn't died, I never would've written the book. He was someone I knew.

**Are all your stories based on something from real life?**

I would say the characters are all based on people as I know them. Sometimes the situations are complete fiction. For instance, in *The Last Book in the Universe*, I've never been to the future, so I had to make it up. But the world of *Freak the Mighty* was right in my backyard.

**When you wrote the dictionary in *Freak the Mighty*, how did you come up with the definitions?**

Originally, the dictionary was just supposed to be there to explain the big words that Kevin used. But when I actually started writing it down, I had a lot of fun coming up with the definitions. Actually, I spent almost as long working on the dictionary pages as I did the whole novel. I guess the words springboard from real words – the kid had a great vocabulary and a great sense of humor, so I tried to combine the two.

**As an adult, how are you able to get inside the head of a kid so well?**

The short answer to that is that I vividly remember being short. I have a very keen recollection of being 11 and 12 years old, and I use my own memories of how I felt at the time to create the characters I'm writing today.

**Did you always want to be a writer when you were growing up?**

At various times, I wanted to be a pilot, because my father had been a pilot; I wanted to be a doctor; I wanted to be President of the United States, but no matter what I wanted to be at any given time, I always assumed I'd also be a writer.

**Did anyone in particular inspire you to become a writer? Parents? Teachers?**

Both of my parents were avid readers. Both of them would've liked to have been writers. But, what really inspired me to become a writer was getting excited by the books I read. That inspired me. It's like if you're a kid and love to watch baseball, it would be natural that you would want to play baseball. It was a very natural thing for me to go from reading to writing.

### Do you have any heroes?

My hero was my father's friend Jack. He was confined to a wheelchair by arthritis as a teenager. He wrote many novels, and none of them were ever published. I never heard him complain about it, he just kept writing. He's my hero.

### How long have you been writing books?

I started writing when I was about 12. I managed to finish a novel-length piece when I was 16 – although it was another 12 years before I finally got a book published!

### What is your favourite part of the writing process? Is it like any other job?

I don't think it's like any other job – sometimes it's easier, sometimes it's harder, but my favourite part is thinking up the stories. Sometimes the writing down part of it is like a regular job. But that's all part of the process. You have to work for anything good.

### Do you ever get writer's block? What do you do when this happens?

I don't really get writer's block, I get lazy. I usually have plenty of ideas, but find that sometimes I don't have the powers of concentration necessary to put them down on paper. So, I do what I always do when I don't know what to write – I go fishing.

What do you mean when you say: "Imagination is a muscle — the more you use it, the stronger it gets"?

I mean that if you want to use your imagination, you have to practise with it. If you wanted to be good at basketball, you'd have to practise shooting baskets. If you want to use your imagination, if you want to be a writer or an artist, or do something creative for a living, you have to use your imagination. You have to use it every day. If you do, it'll get stronger and better, just like an athlete will get stronger and better.

Is there anything else you would like to say to your readers?

Yes. What I always say to my readers:
KEEP READING!!

If you have enjoyed

# FREAK the MIGHTY

You might like to try these
other gripping tales from
Rodman Philbrick...

# Lobster Boy

Skiff Beaman has a problem. A big problem.

He needs to fix up his family's fishing boat but to do that he needs money. A whole heap of money. His father isn't going to help – he can't see further than the next can of beer since Skiff's mother died – and nor is his classmate, Tyler, inventor of the nickname "Lobster Boy".

But Skiff can still hear his mother's voice telling him "Never give up". So he comes up with a plan. It's crazy, it's dangerous, and it's going to take all Skiff's grit and strength to win a great battle against the sea.

"It's the pace, excitement and above all, the inspirational voice of this story that make it unputdownable."

*The Scotsman*

9780746065099

# FIRE PONY

Roy and his big brother, Joe, are on the run from their past when they fetch up at the Bar None ranch. Their shared passion for horses soon wins them great respect, and Roy is offered the chance of a lifetime, to break in a wild pony that runs like the desert wind. He is even promised that if he can ride Lady Luck, he can keep her – a dream come true.

But Roy knows Joe has a dangerous secret...a dark obsession that could explode at any time and send Roy's dream, and their whole world, up in smoke.

"Rodman Philbrick's gripping cowboy story with menace reads like John Steinbeck."

*The Sunday Times*

9780746065082

# THE LAST BOOK
# IN THE UNIVERSE

"Nobody around here reads any more. Why bother, when you can just use a mindprobe needle and shoot all the images and excitement straight into your brain? I've heard of books, but they were long before I was born, in the backtimes before the Big Shake, when everything was supposedly perfect, and everybody lived rich.

In real life, nobody comes to your rescue. Believe me, I know. But then I met Ryter, this old gummy who had a lot of crazy ideas. Together we tried to change the world…"

"Fast-paced and thought provoking… Highly recommended."

*School Librarian*

9780746074398

For more inspirational reads, log on to
www.fiction.usborne.com